LEA

PASCAL MERCIER was born in 1944 in Switzerland. He is the author of several novels, including the international bestseller, *Night Train to Lisbon*. He currently lives in Berlin, where he is a professor of philosophy.

LEA

PASCAL MERCIER

Translated from the German by
SHAUN WHITESIDE

Atlantic Books
LONDON

First published as *Lea* in Germany in 2007 by Carl Hanser Verlag.

First published in trade paperback in Great Britain in 2017 by Atlantic Books, an imprint of Atlantic Books Ltd.

10 9 8 7 6 5 4 3 2 1

A CIP catalogue record for this book is available from the British Library.

Trade Paperback ISBN: 978 1 84887 341 4
OME ISBN: 978 1 78649 072 8
E-book ISBN: 978 1 78239 982 7

Text designed and set in Plantin by Tetragon, London.
Printed and bound by MBM Print SCS Ltd, Glasgow.

Atlantic Books
An Imprint of Atlantic Books Ltd
Ormond House
26–27 Boswell Street
London
WC1N 3JZ

www.atlantic-books.co.uk

LEA

WE CAST THE SHADOWS OF OUR EMOTIONS
ON OTHERS AND THEY THEIRS ON US

SOMETIMES WE THREATEN
TO CHOKE ON THEM

BUT WITHOUT THEM THERE WOULD
BE NO LIGHT IN OUR LIVES

Ancient Armenian grave inscription

1

We first met one bright, windy morning in Provence. I was sitting outside a café in Saint-Rémy, studying the branches of the bare plane trees in the pale light. The waiter who had brought me my coffee was standing in the doorway. In his worn-out, red waistcoat he looked as if he had been a waiter his whole life. Every now and again he took a drag on his cigarette. Once he waved to a girl who was sitting side-saddle on the back of a rattling Vespa, like in an old film from my schooldays. After the Vespa had disappeared, the smile stayed on his lips for a while. I thought about the clinic where things were carrying on without me for the third week. Then I looked across at the waiter again. His face was closed now and his expression blank. I wondered what it would have been like to live his life instead of mine.

At first Martijn van Vliet was a shock of grey hair in a red Peugeot with Bern plates. He was trying to park, and even though there was plenty of room he was making a poor job of it. This uncertainty about parking didn't match the tall man who now got out and strode confidently through the traffic towards the café. He glanced at me sceptically with his dark eyes and walked inside.

Tom Courtenay, I thought. Tom Courtenay in *The Loneliness of the Long Distance Runner*. That was who the man reminded me of. But he didn't look like him at all. The two men resembled one another in their gait and their expression – the way they seemed to be in the world and within themselves. The headmaster of the college hates Tom Courtenay, the gangly boy with the sly smile, but he needs him to win against the other college with its star runner. So he is allowed to run during class time. He runs and runs through the colourful autumn foliage, the camera on his happy, smiling face. The day comes, Tom Courtenay runs far ahead of the rest, his rival looks as if he has been paralysed, Courtenay turns into the home straight, close-up of the headmaster's fat face, beaming with anticipated triumph, only another hundred yards to victory, another fifty, then Courtenay becomes infuriatingly slow, puts the brakes on and stops, incredulity on the headmaster's face, now he recognizes the intention, the boy has him in the palm of his hand, this is his revenge for all the bullying, he sits down on the ground, shakes out his legs, which could have gone on running for ages, his rival runs across the finishing line and Courtenay's face twists into a triumphant grin. I had to see that grin over and over again in the lunchtime showing, in the afternoon and evening and in the late show on Saturday.

A grin like that could appear on the face of this man too, I thought, when Van Vliet came out and sat down at the next table. He put a cigarette between his lips and shielded the flame of the lighter against the wind with his hand. He held the smoke in his lungs for a long time. As he exhaled he glanced at me, and I was at amazed at how gentle those eyes could be.

'*Froid*,' he said and pulled his jacket tighter. '*Le vent*.' He said it with the same accent as I would use.

'Yes,' I said with a Bernese inflection, 'I wouldn't have expected that here. Not even in January.'

Something in his face changed. It wasn't a pleasant surprise for him to meet a Swiss person here. I felt intrusive.

'No, in fact,' he said now, also in dialect, 'it's often like this.' His eyes drifted across the street. 'I can't see a Swiss registration number.'

'I'm here in a hire car,' I said. 'I'm taking the train back to Bern tomorrow.'

The waiter brought him a Pernod. For a while neither of us said anything. The rattling Vespa with the girl on the back seat drove past. The waiter waved.

I set the money for the coffee on the table and started to go.

'I'm driving back tomorrow too,' Van Vliet said now. 'We could go together.'

That was the last thing I had expected. He could see that.

'Just an idea,' he said, and a strangely sad smile, asking for forgiveness, darted across his features; now, once again, he was the man who had parked so maladroitly. Before going to sleep I thought that Tom Courtenay could smile like that too, and in the dream that's exactly what he did. He brought his lips close to the mouth of a girl who recoiled in horror. '*Just an idea, you know*,' said Courtenay, '*and not much of an idea, either*.'

'Yes, why not?' I said now.

Van Vliet called the waiter and ordered two Pernods. I gestured that I didn't want one. A surgeon doesn't drink in the morning; not even after he's stopped work. I sat down at his table.

'Van Vliet,' he said. 'Martijn van Vliet.'

I held out my hand. 'Herzog, Adrian Herzog.'

He'd been staying here only for a few days, he said, and after a pause during which his face seemed to become older and darker, he added: 'In memory of . . . before.'

At some point on our journey he would tell me the story. It would be a sad story, a story that hurt. I had the feeling I wouldn't be up to it. I had enough on my plate dealing with myself.

I gazed along the avenue of plane trees that led out of the town and looked at the mild, muted colours of Provence in winter. I had come here to visit my daughter, who was working at the hospital in Avignon. My daughter who no longer needed me, hadn't done for ages. 'Taken early retirement? You?' she had said. I had hoped she would want to know more. But then the boy had come home from school. Leslie was annoyed that the nanny was late, because she was on the night-shift, and then we were standing in the street like two people who had encountered one another without really meeting.

She saw that I was disappointed. 'I'll visit you,' she said. 'You've got time now!' We both knew she wouldn't. She hasn't been to Bern for many years and doesn't know how I live. We know very little about each other generally, my daughter and I.

I'd hired a car at Avignon Station and had driven off at random, three days on small roads, spending the night in rural inns, half a day by the Gulf of Aigues-Mortes, sandwiches and coffee, time and time again, Somerset Maugham in the evening by dim light. Sometimes I was able to forget the boy who had suddenly appeared in front of the car back then, but never for longer than half a day. I started from my sleep, because anxious sweat was pouring over my eyes and I was nearly choking behind my surgical mask.

'You do it, Paul,' I had said to the senior doctor and handed him the scalpel.

Now, as I drove through the villages at a walking pace and was glad when I was on the open road again, I sometimes saw Paul's bright eyes above the surgical mask, his expression one of shock and disbelief.

I didn't want to hear Martijn van Vliet's story.

'I want to go to the Camargue today, to the Saintes Maries de la Mer,' he said now.

I looked at him. If I hesitated any longer, his expression would harden like Tom Courtenay's when he was standing in front of the headmaster.

'I'll come with you,' I said.

When we set off the wind had stopped and it was warm behind the windscreen. '*La Camargue, c'est le bout du monde,*' said Van Vliet, when we turned south after Arles. 'That's what Cécile, my wife, used to say.'

2

THE FIRST TIME I didn't give it a thought. The second time Van Vliet took his hands off the wheel and held them a few inches away, I thought it was curious, because once again he was doing it while a truck came towards us. But it was only by the third time that I was certain: it was a security measure. He had to keep his hands from doing the wrong thing.

For a while there were no more trucks. On either side of the road were rice fields and water in which the drifting clouds were reflected. The level landscape created the feeling of a liberating expanse. It reminded me of my time in America, when I learned to operate from the very best surgeons. They gave me self-reliance and taught me to master my anxiety, which threatened to break out when I had to make the first incision in the intact skin. By my return to Switzerland in my late thirties I had hazardous operations behind me; for the others I was the epitome of medical calm and confidence, a man who never lost his nerve. It was unimaginable that I would one morning cease to trust myself to hold the scalpel.

In the distance I could see an approaching truck. Van Vliet braked sharply and drove down from the road to a compound with a hotel and a paddock with white horses in it. PROMENADE À CHEVAL, it said by the entrance.

He sat there for a while with his eyes closed. His eyelids twitched and there were fine beads of sweat on his forehead. Then he got silently out of the car and walked slowly over to the paddock fence. I joined him and waited.

'Would you mind taking the wheel?' he asked hoarsely. 'I . . . don't feel that great.'

At the hotel bar he drank two Pernods. Then he said, 'Let's get going.' It was supposed to sound brave, but it was a threadbare courage.

Rather than going to the car he walked back to the paddock. One of the horses was standing by the fence. Van Vliet stroked its head. His hand was trembling.

'Lea loved animals, and they sensed as much. She simply wasn't afraid of them. Even the most furious dogs calmed down when she appeared. "Dad, look, he likes me!" she would cry. As if she needed affection from animals because she didn't experience it otherwise. And she said it to *me*. To me of all people. She stroked the animals, she let them lick her hands. How frightened I was when I saw that! Her precious, her so terribly precious hands. Later, on my secret journeys to Saint-Rémy, I often stood here and imagined her stroking the horses. It would have done her good. I'm quite sure it would have done. But I couldn't bring her along. The Maghrebi, the damned Maghrebi, he forbade it. He simply forbade me to do it.'

I was still frightened of the story, even more so now; none the less, I was no longer certain that I didn't want to hear it. Van Vliet's trembling hand on the horse's head had changed things. I wondered whether I should ask questions. But it would have been wrong. I needed to be a listener, nothing more than a listener, quietly making my way into the world of his thoughts.

He mutely handed me the car key. His hand was still trembling.

I drove slowly. When we met a lorry, Van Vliet looked far into the distance on the right-hand side. As we entered the town, he directed me towards the beach. We stopped behind the dune, walked up the embankment and stepped out on to the sand. It was windy here, the glittering waves broke, and for a moment I thought of Cape Cod and Susan, my then girlfriend.

We walked along, side by side, some distance apart. I didn't know what he was doing here. Or rather I did: now that Lea – about whom he had spoken in the past tense – was no longer alive, he wanted to walk once more along the beach that he had had to walk along alone when the Maghrebi had forbidden him access to his daughter. Now he walked towards the water, and for a moment I had the idea that he was simply going to walk into it, with a straight, solid stride, not to be stopped by anything, further and further, until the waves closed over his head.

He stopped on the damp sand and took a hip flask from his jacket. He unscrewed the top and glanced at me. He hesitated, then threw his head back and poured the spirits down his throat. I got out my camera and took a few photographs. They show him as a silhouette against the light. One of them is here in front of me, leaning against the lamp. I love it. A man drinking defiantly in front of the eyes of another man, who didn't want a Pernod when he was offered one. *Je m'en fous*, says the posture of this tall, heavy, tousle-haired man. Like Tom Courtenay marching off to be arrested after refusing to apologize.

Van Vliet walked on along the damp sand for a while. Every now and again he paused, threw his head back, as he had done while drinking a moment before, and held his face into the sun. A man, perhaps in his late fifties, tanned and his eyes baggy from drinking, but otherwise looking healthy and fit, someone you would have expected to do sport, but behind that appearance filled with grief and despair that could turn at any time into rage and hatred, hatred not least for himself, a man who no longer trusted his hands when he saw the high bonnet of a lorry thundering towards him.

Now he came slowly up to me and stopped right in front of me. The way it came pouring out of him proved how much the memory had raged within him when he was standing by the water.

'Meridjen is his name, the Maghrebi, Dr Meridjen. *Now it's all about your daughter. You will have to get used to it*. Imagine. That's what the man dared to say to me. To me! *C'est de votre fille qu'il s'agit*. As if that hadn't been the guiding principle of my life for twenty-seven years! The words pursued me like an endless echo. He uttered them at the end of our first conversation, before he stood up behind his desk to walk me to the door of his consulting room. He had mostly listened; every now and again the dark hand with the silver pen had flown over the paper. In the ceiling the huge blades of a fan turned wearily; during the pauses in our conversation I heard the quiet humming of the engine. After my long report I felt drained, and when he cast one of his black, Arab looks at me over the lenses of his half-rimmed glasses, I felt as if I were the guilty party sitting before a judge.

'*You aren't moving to Saint-Rémy*, he said to me in the doorway. It was a devastating sentence. Those few words made it sound as if my devotion to what I saw as Lea's happiness was nothing but an orgy of paternal ambition and a desperate attempt to bind her to me. As if my daughter needed to be protected from me more than anything. When I had only this one desire for Lea, this one desire that swept all others aside: that her grief and despair about Cécile's death might be over for ever. Of course, that desire also concerned *me*. *Of course* it did. But who would reproach me for that? *Who*?'

There were tears in his eyes. I would have loved to run my hand through his windswept hair. How had it all come about? I asked, after we had sat down in the sand beside the embankment.

3

'I CAN TELL YOU to the day, indeed the hour, precisely when it all began. It was a Tuesday eighteen years ago, the only weekday when Lea's school continued into the afternoon. A day in May, deep blue, with trees and shrubs blossoming all around. Lea came out of school, with Caroline beside her, her friend from her earliest schooldays. It hurt to see how sadly and stiffly Lea came down the few steps to the playground next to skipping Caroline. It was the same dragging walk as it had been a year ago, when we had come together out of the hospital where Cécile had lost her battle against leukaemia. That day, saying goodbye to her mother's unmoving face, Lea had stopped crying. Her tears were used up. In the last weeks leading up to that moment she had talked less and less, and with every day, it seemed to me, her movements had become slower and jerkier.

Nothing had been able to loosen that stiffness: nothing that I had done with her; none of the many presents I had bought when it seemed to me that I could read a desire in her face; none of the awkward jokes that I wrested from my own stiffness; not even going to school, with all the new impressions that it brought; and not even the efforts that Caroline had made from the first day onwards to make her laugh.

'"*Adieu,*" Caroline said to Lea at the gate and put her arm around her shoulder. For an eight-year-old girl it was an unusual gesture: as if she were the adult sister giving the younger one protection and consolation to take with her on her way. As always, Lea kept her eyes fixed on the floor and didn't reply. She silently put her hand in mine and walked along beside me as if wading through lead.

'We had just walked past the Schweizerhof Hotel and were approaching the escalator that leads down to the station hall, when Lea froze in the middle of the stream of people. In my mind I was already in the difficult meeting that I would shortly have to chair, and I tugged impatiently on her hand. She suddenly twisted away, stood there for a few moments with her head lowered, and then ran towards the escalator. Even today I can see her running, slaloming through the hurrying crowd, the wide satchel on her narrow back catching more than once in other people's clothes. When I caught up with her she was standing with her neck craning at the top of the escalator, heedless of the people whose way she was blocking. "*Écoute!*" she said as I walked over to her. She said it in the same tone as Cécile, who had always voiced the demand in

French, even though we spoke German the rest of the time. To someone like me, whose throat is not made for bright French sounds, the sharp word had a commanding, dictatorial tone that intimidated me, even if it concerned something harmless. So I reined in my impatience and listened obediently to the station hall below. Now I, too, heard what had made Lea pause: the sound of a violin. Hesitantly I let her drag me on to the escalator and now we slid – against my will, in fact – down towards the hall of Bern Station.

'How often have I wondered what would have become of my daughter if we hadn't done that! If chance had not played those sounds to us. If I had given in to the strain and impatience of the impending meeting and dragged Lea on with me. Would she have yielded to the fascination of the sound of the violin on another occasion, in another form? What else would one day have freed her from her paralysing grief? Would her talent have come to light in any case? Or would she have become a very ordinary schoolgirl with a very ordinary career aspiration? And what about me? Where would I be now if I hadn't found myself faced with the monstrous challenge of Lea's gift, for which I was by no means a match?

'When we stepped on to the escalator that afternoon, I was a forty-year-old biocyberneticist, the youngest member of the faculty and, as people said, a rising star in the firmament of this new discipline. Cécile's last days and her early death had shocked me, more profoundly than I was willing to admit. But outwardly I had withstood that shock, and through meticulous planning had succeeded in linking my job with my role as a father who now held sole responsibility. At night, when I sat at my computer, I heard Lea tossing and turning in the next room, and I myself didn't go to sleep until she had come to rest, regardless of how late it got. I fought the fatigue, which grew like a creeping poison, with coffee, and sometimes I was on the brink of taking up smoking again. But I didn't want Lea growing up in a smoky flat with an addicted father.'

Van Vliet took the cigarettes out of his jacket and lit one. As he had done that morning in the café, he screened the flame against the wind with his big hand. Now, from closer up, I saw the nicotine on his fingers.

'All in all I had the situation under control, or so it seemed to me; only the rings under my eyes were growing bigger and darker. I think everything could have turned out all right if the two of us hadn't stepped on to the escalator. But Lea already had one foot on the sliding metal – when she was so afraid of escalators, a fear she inherited from Cécile; so much had entered her from her idolized mother, as if by osmosis. At that moment the music was stronger than her fear, that was why she had taken the first step, and now I couldn't leave her alone and ran my hand soothingly over her hair until we had reached the bottom and plunged into the crowd of breathless people listening, enchanted, to the violinist.'

Van Vliet threw the half-smoked cigarette into the sand and hid his face in his hands. He was standing beside his little daughter in the station. It cut me to the quick. I thought of my visit to Leslie in Avignon. Leslie had never been to me what Lea had been to Martijn van Vliet. We had had a more sober relationship. Not unloving, but more brittle. Was it because in the years after she was born I had done almost nothing but work, and often not emerged from the hospital in Boston for days at a time?

That was how Joanne put it. *As a father you're a failure.*

We hadn't had a single proper holiday; if I travelled, it was to conferences where new surgical techniques were being presented. Leslie was nine when we came back to Switzerland. She spoke a mixture of Joanne's American and my Bern German. The tensions between her parents closed her off from us. She looked for friends that we didn't know, and when Joanne went back to America for ever, Leslie went to boarding school – a good one, but still a boarding school. I don't think she was unhappy, but she was slipping further and further away from me, and when I saw her it was more of a meeting between two good acquaintances than between father and daughter.

Van Vliet's story would be the story of a misfortune, that much was clear; but that misfortune had grown out of a happiness that I had never known, whatever the reason.

'She wasn't a tall woman,' he said, interrupting my thoughts, 'but she was standing on a pedestal and her torso loomed over the crowd. And, my God, you would have fallen in love with her on the spot! The way you can fall in love with an overwhelmingly beautiful statue, but more easily, more quickly and much, much more intensely. The first thing that had caught my eye was a torrent of gleaming black hair that seemed to flow once more from her pale, three-cornered hat and down on to the padded shoulders of her frock coat. And what a fairy-tale frock coat it was! Faded pink and washed-out yellow, the colours of a decaying palazzo. Against it there stood out many twisting dragon figures, red-gold threads and red glass splinters that shimmered like priceless rubies. There was much of the mysterious East in that jacket, which reached almost to the woman's knees. She wore it open; you could see a pair of beige knee britches, which were held at the top by an ochre-coloured scarf, with white silk stockings in black patent shoes. Above the scarf she wore a ruched blouse of white satin that filled the wide stand-up collar with a collar of its own. She had drawn a piece of the soft white fabric over the stand-up collar, and on it her energetic chin pressed down on the violin. And to top it all, the broad hat with the three corners, its material similar to the frock coat, but heavier in effect because the edges were lined with black velvet. We made countless drawings of her together, Lea and I, and could never agree about some of the details.' Van Vliet gulped. 'That was in the kitchen, at the big table that Cécile had brought to our marriage.'

He got to his feet, without an explanation, and went to the water. A wave washed over his shoes and he didn't seem to notice.

'It isn't quite right,' he went on as he sat down beside me again, with seaweed on his shoes, 'to say that the long wavy hair was what first thrilled me about that violinist. Even more than that it was her eyes – or rather not her eyes but the white mask that merged almost seamlessly with her white powdered face. The longer I stood there, the more I fell under the spell of the masked face. At first it was the stillness and the sheer materiality of the mask that struck me, because they contrasted so starkly with the soulful music. How could a stiff mask produce something like that? Gradually I began to sense the eyes behind the little slits, and then to see them. Usually they were closed, and then the powdered face looked sealed-off and dead. Then the sounds seemed to come almost from another world and to use her sightless body like a medium. Particularly in slow, lyrical passages, when the instrument barely moved and the arm with the bow slipped only slowly through space. It was a little as if God's wordless voice were speaking to the breathlessly listening travellers who had set their suitcases, backpacks and bags on the floor beside them, and were absorbing the overwhelming music as a revelation. The other sounds of the station seemed to lack reality compared to the music. The sounds coming out of the darkly gleaming violin had a reality of their own, which, it occurred to me, could not have been shaken even by an explosion.

'Now and again the woman opened her eyes. When she did that I was reminded of films featuring masked bank robbers, which always filled me with a burning desire to know what the face belonging to the eyes might look like. Throughout all that time, in my mind I was taking off the violinist's mask and imagining expressions and whole faces for her. I wondered what it would be like to sit facing such eyes and such a face over dinner or engage in conversation. I only learned that she was mute, this mysterious princess of the violin, from reading the newspaper. I didn't tell Lea. Nor did she learn anything about the rumour that the woman wore a mask because her face was disfigured by burns. I only told her of the woman's supposed name: LOYOLA DE COLÓN. After that I had to tell her all about Ignatius of Loyola and Christopher Columbus. She soon forgot it; she was only concerned with the name. Later I bought her a beautiful edition of the *Complete Works* of Saint Ignatius. She placed it in such a way that she could see the book from her bed. She never read it.

'Loyola – that was what we called her later, as if she were an old friend – was playing Bach's Partita in E major. I didn't know that at the time – until then music hadn't been something with which I had seriously engaged. Now and again Cécile had dragged me to a concert, but I behaved like the caricature of a blinkered science geek and artistic philistine. It was my little daughter who introduced me to the universe of music, and with my methodically ticking intelligence, my scientist's intelligence, I learned all about it, without knowing whether I loved the music that she played because I liked it or whether it was just because it seemed to belong to Lea's happiness. Today I know the Bach Partita, which she would later play with more depth and brilliance than anyone else – to my ears, at least – as well as if I had written it myself. If only I could wipe it from my memory!

'I can't remember how good Loyola's violin was. At the time I had no idea, I became an expert in violin tones only on my insane journey to Cremona, many years later. But in my memory, which would soon be overlaid and transformed by the imagination, that fateful instrument had a warm, voluminous, intoxicating, addictive sound. That sound, which suited the aura of the masked woman so well, and her eyes, as I imagined them, had made me forget Lea for a moment, even though her hand had been in mine as always when she was surrounded by lots of people. Now I sensed her hand twisting away from mine and I was amazed at how damp it was.

'Her damp hands and her concern for her hands: how they would determine the future – and for a time darken it!

'I still had no idea that this would come about, when I looked down at her and saw her eyes, to which something incredible had happened. Lea held her hand tilted to one side to get a better view of the violinist through a narrow gap in the crowd. The sinews in her neck were tested to breaking point. She had become her gaze. And her eyes shone!

'In the long period of our hospital visits to Cécile, they had gone out and lost the gleam that we had loved so much. With eyes lowered and shoulders drooping she had stood in silence by the grave as the coffin was lowered into the ground. Back then, when I felt my breath catching and my eyes starting to sting, I couldn't have said whether it was more because of Cécile or more because of the horribly mute grief and abandonment that spoke from Lea's dull eyes. And now, more than a year later, their gleam had returned.

'I looked again in disbelief, and again. But the new gleam was actually there, it was real, and it made it look as if the heavens had suddenly opened up for my daughter. Her body, her whole body, was tense to bursting, and her clenched knuckles stood out like little white hills against the rest of her skin. It was as if she had to summon all of her strength to resist the enchanting power of the music. In retrospect, it seems to me as if with that tension she had been preparing for her new life, which was beginning during those minutes – as if she had been tensed like a runner before a sprint, the run of her life.

'And then, all of a sudden, the tension relaxed, her shoulders sank and her arms dangled at her side – forgotten, unfeeling appendages. For a moment I thought it was the extinction of her interest that was expressed in this sudden slackening, and feared that she had fallen out of her enchantment, back into the desperate jadedness of the past year. But then I saw an expression in her eyes that didn't match it, but pointed in the other direction. It was still a gleam, but there was something mixed in with it, something that startled me even though I didn't understand it: something in Lea's soul had decided to take over the governance of her life. And I felt, with a mixture of apprehension and happiness, that my own life would also be drawn into the spell of that mysterious control, and would never again be as it was before.

'If Lea had previously breathed, during times of tension, in irregular bursts that made one think of a fever, for which the red patches on her cheeks were a match, now she no longer seemed to be breathing at all, and her slack face was covered with an alabaster, corpse-like pallor. If her eyelids had previously twitched frantically, now they seemed paralysed.

At the same time there was also concentrated intention in her motionlessness – as if Lea were reluctant to let them interrupt her gaze upon the playing goddess, even if those interruptions had lasted only a few hundredths of a second, and she wouldn't have noticed them in any case.

'In the light of what happened later, and what I know now, I would say: I lost my daughter in that station hall.

'I would say it, even though over the next few years it looked as if precisely the opposite had happened: as if at that moment she had unwittingly started on a journey towards herself, and with a devotion, a fervour and energy that very few can manage. Exhaustion lay on the pale features of her childish face, and when I sometimes dreamed of that exhaustion, it was the exhaustion that lay before her on her self-sacrificing journey through the world of sounds, which she would walk along in a consuming fever.

'The woman's playing came to an end with a spirited, rather dramatic stroke of the bow. A silence that swallowed up all the noise of the station. Then thunderous applause. Her bows were deep and lasted for an unusually long time. She held her violin and bow far from her body, as if to protect it from her own impetuous movements. The hat must have been fastened on, because it stayed where it was while the surge of black hair poured forwards, burying her face beneath it. When she straightened, her hair flew back as if in a storm, the hand holding the bow brushed the strands of hair from her face, and now the white face with the mask was a real shock, even though we had had it in front of our eyes all along. We wanted to see joy on the face, or exhaustion, or at least some kind of emotional reaction; instead our gaze bounced back off the ghostly mask and the powder. Still, it seemed as if the applause would never end. Very slowly the crowd began moving and divided into those who were in a hurry and the others who were queuing up to throw something into the violin case beside the podium. Some looked in astonishment at their watches and seemed to be wondering where the time had gone.

'Lea stayed where she was. Nothing about her had changed, her trance continued, and it was still as if her eyelids had ceased to function, so overwhelmed were they by what her eyes had seen. There was something infinitely touching in her refusal to believe that it was over. The desire for it to continue, to continue for ever, was so strong that she didn't even snap out of it when jostled by a commuter in a hurry. She stayed in her new position with the unconscious certainty of a sleepwalker, her gaze still fixed on Loyola, as if she were a marionette that she could force to move simply by looking at her. This unwavering gaze of Lea's heralded her unique and finally destructive firmness of will, which would come to light more and more clearly over the next few years.

'Loyola, it turned out now, was not alone. A tall, dark-skinned man suddenly moved in. He took her violin and bow away, held out his hand as she stepped down from the podium, then cleared everything away with a skill and swiftness that surprised others besides myself. Barely more than two or three minutes seemed to have passed since the last coin had fallen in the case, and Loyola was already making for the escalator with her companion. Now that she was no longer standing on a podium, she looked small, the magical violinist, and not only small, but stripped of her enchantment, almost a little shabby. She dragged one leg, and I was ashamed of my disappointment at discovering that she was real and imperfect, rather than moving through the world with the same lustre, the same fairy-tale perfection that her playing had possessed. I was glad and unhappy at once when the escalator carried them up and out of our field of vision.

'I walked over to Lea and drew her gently to me, the same movement as ever when I needed to console and protect her. Then she would press her cheek to my hip, and if things were particularly bad she would bury her face in me. Now, however, it was different, and even though it was only a small movement, a mere nuance in her reaction, it still changed the world. Under the gentle pressure of my hand Lea slowly returned to reality. At first she yielded, as she normally did, to my protective gesture. But then, for a tiny moment, she paused abruptly and began to resist me.

'I sensed what was happening, and it hit me like an electric shock: while she had been immersed in herself a new will had formed, a new independence had come into being, one of which she was still unaware.

'I drew my hand back with a start, fearfully waiting for what would happen next. Since coming to, Lea had not yet looked at me. When our eyes met now, it was for a moment which I experienced with unnatural alertness, like the encounter between two adults with matching wills. The person standing here was no longer a little daughter in need of protection, facing her tall, protective father, but a young woman filled with a will and a future for which she demanded unconditional respect.

'At that moment I sensed that a new calendar was beginning between us.

'But new and clear though that sensation was – I plainly understood it neither then nor later. *C'est de votre fille qu'il s'agit.* What could those terrible words of the Maghrebi mean other than the accusation that in the thirteen years since Loyola's appearance at Bern Station it had never really been about Lea, but only ever about me? In the first days and weeks I refused – I grimly, bitterly refused – to consider the accusation seriously for so much as a moment. But the doctor's words circled and circled, they poisoned my sleeping and my waking, until I grew tired of resisting and tried with all the sobriety of my intellect to approach myself entirely from outside, as if approaching a stranger. Had I perhaps really been incapable of acknowledging that Lea had a will of her own, which might be a will other than the one I dreamed of for her?

'It never occurred to me that I might be trapped in such fatal impotence; because if it had taken control of me, it was with a sly discretion, a treacherous mutability, which eluded the discerning gaze and concealed itself behind the deceptive façade of solicitude. To the casual observer, in fact, it didn't look as if I was ignoring what Lea wished for herself. Quite the contrary: from outside it must have looked as if – from month to month, year to year – I was increasingly becoming the servant, indeed the slave, of her wishes. The occasional glance from my colleagues and co-workers told me that they were concerned about the degree to which I allowed the form of my life to be dictated by the rhythm of Lea's life, her artistic advances and setbacks, her highs and her lows, her euphoria and her depression, her moods and her illnesses. And how could anyone deny a father his capacity, even if he sometimes found himself on the wrong track for the sake of his daughter, to acknowledge her will? I eagerly fell in with the tyranny of her gift. So how could the Maghrebi question my readiness to acknowledge Lea as a person in her own right? And how could he give me to understand, with his gently dictatorial manner, that it was this incapacity of mine that had made her his patient? *You aren't moving to Saint-Rémy*. Good God!'

4

VAN VLIET HAD got to his feet and was preparing to go to the water again. His clenched fists could be seen in his jacket pocket. I went along. He took out his hip flask, hesitated and glanced at me. I caught his eye and held it. His thumb rubbed on the flask.

'But I'd like to hear more of the story,' I said.

A skewed smile appeared on his face. Tom Courtenay wouldn't have had cause for such a smile, but it would also have been impossible on Courtenay's face.

'OK,' said Van Vliet, and put the flask back in his pocket.

A man with a Newfoundland dog came towards us. The dog ran ahead and stopped, panting, in front of us. Van Vliet stroked its head and let it lick his hand. We didn't look at each other, but we both knew that we were thinking about

Lea and the animals. The way our thoughts interlocked: had I ever experienced that with Joanne or with Leslie? And I had known Martijn van Vliet for less than half a day.

The dog ran away and Van Vliet wiped his hand on his trousers. We walked over to the water. The wind had subsided, the waves just lapped quietly now.

'Lea loved it when the sea was as smooth as a mirror. It reminded her of the ringing of the bell in a Japanese monastery, early in the morning. She liked films like that. And comparisons like that. Once, during the Olympic Games in Seoul, I turned on the television late at night. The Koreans call their country *The Land of Morning Silence*, the reporter said. Lea had stepped up behind me, silently, on bare feet, sleepless after so much practising. 'How lovely,' she said. We looked at the rowing boats cutting through the smooth water. That was a few months after Loyola's performance in the station.'

He took a quick slug from the flask.

His movements were mechanical, without his intervention, behind them he had already yielded once more to the flow of memory.

'Lea looked over at the escalator on which the violinist had disappeared, started walking and her foot buckled. It was as if she had started walking before her body was entirely back in her possession after her dreamy absence. She hobbled and her face was distorted with pain, but it was not defiant and stubborn as it had been recently when something had hurt her; it was more of a distracted expression which made the pain seem more like something mildly troublesome than something that deserved attention. I have dreamed of that buckled foot. I held Lea's leg like a doctor, but one who was also partly responsible for the accident. The dream lasted much longer than the harmless twisted ankle, which healed quickly. But in the end, when Lea blossomed, it disappeared. With my stolen visits to the hospice gardens of Saint-Rémy it came back. I do nothing in the dream, I just see Lea hobbling past some distance away, her age is vague, her face is strange, and I awaken with the feeling of having been witness to some deep damage to her life. *Elle est brisée dans son âme*, said the Maghrebi.

'How different things looked that evening after Loyola's concert! We walked together through the city. We had never walked through Bern like that before. It was as if we were walking outside of town, separated from the stone of the arcades and the rest of reality by a gap, a tiny hiatus that made it look as if the thousand familiar things had nothing to do with us in the slightest. The only thing that counted was that Lea was walking as she had not walked for ages, liberated and resolute, and that by doing so she kindled within me the hope that her soul might be reawakened and made to flow by the music.

'She hobbled, but she seemed to pay it no heed. Her constant disregard for the pain made her walk assertively, in a way that left no doubt that she was the one deciding where we went. For a long time we didn't say a word. She led me mutely down streets and alleys that I had not walked down for years. A mysterious, inexhaustible power seemed to impel her onwards, and her gaze, fixed on the cobbles, kept me from asking her what her goal might be. Only once did I ask: "Where are we going?" She didn't look at me, but said as if out of the deepest concentration, "*Viens!*" It sounded like the order of someone who has over her fellow the knowledge of something great, without wishing to explain it.

'Flooding through my head came those many occasions when Cécile, too, had said such a "*Viens!*" to me, with gentle, compelling impatience. How I had enjoyed it at first when she did it! Someone taking me by the hand and leading me along – how unfamiliar and liberating it had been for someone who, as a latchkey child, had been forced far too early to make his way alone to school and in the street, dogged in his devious intelligence, the only thing he trusted.

'Our ghostly walk, which Lea's impatient energy sometimes turned into almost a march, lasted over an hour, and when my eye caught a church clock I was hotly aware of the session that I was supposed to have been leading. It was a crucial meeting with donors and the university management – the future of my lab depended on it; so it was unthinkable that I should not be there. The thought of the staff members who would helplessly have to endure questioning glances made me start from my oblivious present, which had consisted entirely of being Lea's companion. I saw a telephone box and looked in my jacket pocket for coins. But then again I sensed Lea's mysterious energy beside me, and now I made a decision of a kind that I would make again and again in the coming years: I gave my daughter precedence over my professional duties and shut my eyes to the consequences that became more threatening every time. Her will, wherever it might drive us both, meant more to me than anything else. Her life was more important than mine. The Maghrebi knows nothing of that. *Nothing*.

'I had dropped back behind Lea, and now caught up with her. We started to walk in a circle, and gradually it dawned on me that she didn't have a goal at all, or rather that her goal was not one that you could walk to. She walked along beside me as if she actually wished she were walking to somewhere quite different, but didn't know where, and more than that: as if she would rather have been moving in a quite different, more significant space than the one that Bern old town made available.

'Now we were walking past Krompholz, the music shop. Lea – and this surprises me even today – didn't glance once at the window, where a number of violins were always displayed. She walked heedlessly past, even though, as I would learn shortly, something was stirring in her soul that would give such instruments a life-defining significance. My own eyes ran over the violins and connected them with the woman from the station – in the way that one's ideas normally connect. As yet I had no idea what violins would mean for both our lives. That they would change everything.

'Then, all of a sudden, all the energy seemed to drain from Lea. The pain in her ankle must have become greater and greater, and where before she had impelled me onwards with mute, dictatorial resolution, now she was only a tired little girl whose foot hurt and who wanted to go home.

'Arriving at our flat seemed different. I felt a little as if we had just been on a long journey: I was surprised at all the furniture there, its practicality seemed dubious to me, the cunningly calculated light from the many lamps suddenly didn't match my expectations, and it smelled of dust and stale air. The many things that recalled Cécile seemed to have been pushed further into the past, as if by an imperceptible shove. I put a compression dressing on Lea's swollen joint. She didn't eat anything, poked around absently in the saffron rice, her favourite meal. Then, suddenly, she raised her eyes and looked at me the way you look at someone you're about to ask a vitally important question.

'"Is a violin expensive?"

'These four words, spoken in the childish tone of her bright voice – I will hear them until the end of my life. All at once it was clear to me what had happened in her, and what had provoked the unease of our strange and opaque walk through the city: she had sensed that she, too, wanted to be able to do what the violinist in the fairy-tale costume could do. The aimlessness that had accompanied her grief over her dead mother had come to an end. She had a *will* again! And what made me overjoyed: I could *do* something. The time of being a helpless onlooker was over.

'"There are very expensive violins, which only rich people can afford," I said, "but there are others, too. Would you like to have one?"

'I stayed in my chair in the sitting room until I heard Lea's calm breathing. And while I sat there, something happened that later slipped from my memory for a long time, to turn up again the day when Lea was collected and taken to the hospital in Saint-Rémy, to the Maghrebi, far from Switzerland and its intrusive press. The sensation that suddenly spread through that sitting room at night was the feeling of losing Cécile. As cruel as it might sound: it had been Lea's leaden grief that had helped me to keep her with me. The mother had become more emphatically present in the daughter's grief than she had sometimes been in life. Now, this evening, after only a few hours during which Lea's grief had begun to make way for a new state of mind, one that was open to the future, Cécile's present also began to fade. I was startled. Had my wife had a present in the end only as Lea's mother?

'I got up, walked through the rooms and touched the things that reminded me of her. I stayed for longest in her room, which, with all the figures and painted shards, could have belonged to an archaeologist. But that had only been a hobby – her dreamy side, which no one who knew her as a determined nurse would have guessed. Lea and I had touched nothing here since her death. Behind closed doors a timeless year had gone by, in which there had been no future that a present could have forced into the past. Lea's question about the violin threatened that sanctuary. At least that was how it seemed to me when I was sitting on the sofa again.

'I would be proved right: not long after the flat began to fill with clumsy, scratching violin sounds, we turned Cécile's room into the music room, *la salle de musique*, as Lea said with proudly and coquettishly pursed lips. We decorated it brightly and in an elegantly antiquated manner, to recall the French and Russian salons in which gifted young musicians played their debuts in front of aristocrats whose stiff and pompous clothing – as we said with a laugh – were like Loyola de Colón's costume. It was wonderful, furnishing Lea's future like that.

'But sometimes I lay awake, choking with grief over the fact that with every advance that my daughter made in the violin she retreated more and more into the past, and grief was mingled with an unreasonable, invisible resentment against Lea for taking away my wife, without whom I would have gone off the rails much sooner.

'Lea was woken by the pain in her foot. I changed the bandage and then we talked about the concert in the station. I learned what I would be forced to learn again and again over the years that followed, however much it hurt: that I had no idea about many things – and precisely about the most important thing – that were going on inside my daughter. That what I thought I knew was only the shadow that my own ideas cast upon her.

'In fact, while I was inventing an almost mystical absorption for her, Lea had been thinking about quite practical things: how Loyola could know where to stop when her hand slid up and down the neck of the violin, and why the narrow wooden bridge didn't dent the wood when there was only a hollow space underneath it and the strings were stretched so tight. We didn't solve either of those mysteries. To the sound of the legendary names of Stradivari, Amati and Guarneri, which I mentioned when we were talking about violins in general, she fell asleep again at last. At the time they were merely radiant, mythical names. If only they had stayed that way. Why did I have to drag them into our life?

'In the uneasy half-sleep of that night I argued with two female figures, superimposed one on the other, distorted and commingled. One of them, who seemed to have threatening power over me and my fate, was Ruth Adamek, my assistant over many years and the deputy director of our laboratory. "You *forgot*?" she had said in disbelief when I explained to her over the telephone why I had missed the meeting and not even called. "You should understand," I said, "Lea had an accident and I couldn't think about anything else." "Is she in hospital?" No, I answered, she was with me. As if it were a confession of guilt, Ruth fell silent for a while. "Wasn't there a phone anywhere nearby? Can you imagine what it was like for us? Just sitting there with those big beasts and not being able to say anything about the fact that you weren't there?" That was how it had been in reality. In my dream she said something else: "Why do you never call? Are you not interested in what I do any more?" Today she is sitting behind my desk, ambitious, competent and with a pair of Cartier glasses on her nose. In my dream, back then, I accused her of selling me a violin whose bridge brought everything crashing down at the first stroke of the bow. My rage was such that I struggled to choke out my furious words. Ruth just left me standing where I was and turned to the next customer. She was working at Krompholz now, and laughed the harsh laugh of the woman who cleaned the lab.'

5

OVER DINNER we laughed about the dream. For the first time we laughed together. Van Vliet's laughter came hesitantly, as if with a preamble of disbelief, and later, when it became more fluid, I was sure: he had had to overcome the feeling of forfeiting the right to laughter. We were sitting outside, in a protected inner courtyard of the restaurant, surrounded by walls whose fresh white gleamed so brightly in the Provençal sun that it hurt. Saintes Maries de la Mer – for that is the place of those bright walls in which I saw Van Vliet laugh.

Would that laughter also have suited Tom Courtenay? Years after I had seen the film, I saw him on stage in London. A comedy. It was good, but that wasn't how I wanted to see him and I left at the interval. It was how I wanted Van Vliet, though, and I wished I could have much more of that laughter. It showed that apart from being Lea's father and the victim of her misfortune he was also someone else, a man of charm and sparkling intelligence. I wished I could put the photograph showing him drinking with the light behind him next to another of his laughing face.

He had composed himself and ordered mineral water, although he also ordered a grappa with his coffee. He wanted to know if I had a wife and children. One might almost have taken the detached way in which he asked for formal politeness, and for a moment I was hurt. But then I understood what it was: self-defence in anticipation. He was afraid of an answer that would show him a man who had had greater good fortune, and had done better with his wife and children.

I said something about my divorce and about the boarding school, but otherwise I didn't find the words to explain to him how things had been with Joanne and how they were with Leslie. So I told him about the boy who had come shooting out of the driveway and was suddenly standing in front of my car. It had been only a matter of inches. My heart hammered all the way home and didn't stop, even on the sofa. I ran to the bathroom and threw up. A sleepless night with camomile tea. I had Sunday off, dozed throughout the day, kept the television on, tried to distract myself. A throbbing headache of the kind I remembered from before my state exam. And then Monday morning in the operating theatre.

'I no longer trusted my hands, my motor memory. What was I supposed to do after the first incision? Where did all the blood go? The nurse silently handed me the scalpel. Seconds passed. I felt the eyes of the others on me. Paul's perplexed eyes above his surgical mask. The throbbing headache on the way home. On long walks I have often stopped and closed my eyes, and my thoughts have gone back to that operating table. The fear of blood didn't go away, it flowed and flowed, the patients bled to death.

'"It's a wonder they don't bleed to death on you," said the schoolmate who had become a psychiatrist. "Why don't you just stop? Didn't you want to become a photographer or a cameraman? Eventually we lose the natural self-evidence of life. Age. Take it as a sign."

'A week later I took early retirement. On my last journey home I tossed the flowers from my farewell party in the bin. I still wake up as early as a surgeon does.'

What I didn't tell him: how I took out the photographs of me from Boston, pictures of a man who was a match for things, the videos of my lectures and operations; the way I examined my face in search of my former certainty; how I gazed in envy at my sure, deft hands, unconcerned with blood; how I suddenly had the feeling that my present agitation was bringing all that had gone before crashing down, the dominoes of the past were falling over, one after the other. It had all been deception. Not a lie, but deception. And I also said nothing about this: how after reserving the hotel in Avignon over the telephone I panicked, because I suddenly thought I had forgotten how to check in and out of a hotel; how I tried out sentences that I needed to say; and how I then lay on the bed in disbelief and thought of all the luxury gaffs I'd stayed in at conferences in India and Hong Kong. Self-confidence: why is it so flighty? Why so blind to the facts? For a lifetime we try to build it up, to secure and consolidate it, knowing that it is the most precious possession and indispensable for happiness. Then, suddenly and with insidious silence, a trapdoor opens, we fall into the abyss and everything that was becomes a *fata Morgana*.

Van Vliet asked what it was like to have a daughter in boarding school. Did you even have the feeling of seeing her grow up? 'Sorry, I'm just trying to imagine.' How often I had visited her. Whether I had experienced her first love, her first heartache. The chaos of emotions when it came to choosing her career.

I was sitting with Leslie beside the boarding school. 'André – it's over,' she had said, and run her handkerchief over her eyes. 'I'd thought it would be nicer; the first time, I mean.' What was it like for you? she wanted to ask, I could see. But there wasn't enough between us for that. 'Doctor,' she said another time and grinned. 'No,' I said. 'Yes,' she said. I think that was the first time we hugged when we said goodbye, and the last.

I had said nothing. 'Sorry,' said Van Vliet. To bring me back, he added a detail from his dream: every time Ruth Adamek picked up a violin, it shrank, so that from that time you could only buy tiny, one-eighth-size violins at Krompholz's shop. Van Vliet liked it when she was ashamed and nervously tugged at her miniskirt. I knew: he didn't dream that, he just invented it to make up for asking me about Leslie.

'The real sales assistant at Krompholz,' he went on, 'was quite unlike Ruth Adamek; and while with each passing year Ruth increasingly became my second fiddle in the institute, in Katharina Walther, the second female figure in that dream, I won a kind of friend with whom I often held conversations in my head when thinking about Lea. When I was the first customer to enter the shop on the morning after Loyola's concert, she came up to me – a woman in her fifties, whose nonchalance struck me most of all in her movements, but was also expressed in a calm, light-grey gaze. An eight-year-old girl, she said, should start with a half-size violin. At around ten she would switch to a three-quarter size and from thirteen or fourteen to a full size. When I showed my puzzlement at the expressions "half-size" and "three-quarter size", I saw for the first time her reticent smile, so good a match for her grey-streaked hair and her severe hairdo with the bun at the back. Later, I sometimes bought certain records just to see that smile.

'The small violin that she brought from the storeroom and set down in front of me was made of pale wood with a delicate, irregular grain. I picked it up as carefully as if any energetic movement might make it crumble to dust. "Wouldn't you like to bring your daughter in, so that we can be sure the size is right?" The woman had known me for just half an hour and already she had hit the bullseye. Certainly, it was a good, natural practical question. But in retrospect it seems to me that she sensed I was making a mistake that went far beyond anything practical. Even today I can see how she raised her eyebrows when I hesitated. It would all have been different if I had understood the lesson that this worldly woman gave me that morning in the empty shop. Instead I said, and it must have sounded like a hasty decision: "I want to surprise Lea." Then I paid the first instalment on the violin. "If there's anything else, just drop in with Lea," the woman said and gave me her card.

'The fact that she had mentioned Lea by name echoed inside me. When I stepped out of the shop with the little violin case, I had the feeling that I had never held anything so precious in my hands. I gave a start when a passer-by bumped into the case and for the rest of the journey I held it anxiously in front of my chest.

'In that posture I entered the institute. No one paid the violin the slightest attention. How were my colleagues supposed to know that it was the symbol of Lea's reawakening into life? None the less – I took it amiss of them for not asking a single question or making a single remark about this precious object, but sitting there in silence and waiting for an explanation for my inexcusable absence. That silence made them my enemies.

'They would hear no voluntary explanation or apology from me. That was what I decided when I was sitting in my office and looking across the city at the Alps. The snow-covered, majestic mountains loomed into the evenly deep-blue sky like the bright green meadows that I had been watching yesterday outside Lea's school. Less than twenty-four hours had passed since then, and yet the world had changed.

'In front of me was a note from my secretary about a call from the rector, summoning me in to see him. A short time later, in a gleaming chrome university office full of electronics I turned myself back into the unruly schoolboy I had once been, who refused to be intimidated by any threats, who took out his pocket chess during lessons in spite of every kind of warning, because he caught up in a flash on the backlog created by his truancy, to be top once again in the crucial tests. Back then I lied right, left and centre, and it was like a chess game: you always had to be one step ahead of the others. I would do the same thing today if it was a matter of defending Lea against the rest. She could rely on that.

'The rector couldn't have known that he was sitting opposite a colleague in whom the cold-bloodedly lying ragamuffin of former times had just reawakened. I think he was surprised by the shortness and abruptness of my invented story about Lea's accident, and how little it sounded like an apology. But he had no other choice but to believe me, and in the end we fixed a date for a new meeting with the donors.

'My dereliction was forgotten. What was left was a certain coolness between my colleagues and me. Every now and again Ruth tried to find fault with me; but I was on my guard, and always one step ahead of her rancour. As I say: you can rely on it.'

6

'LEA'S TRANSFORMATION was like a silent explosion. That evening, when she stood staring at the violin case that I had laid open on her bed, there were no exclamations of surprise, no expressions of ecstasy, no jumping in the air, no transport of joy. In fact, nothing happened at all. Lea picked up the violin and started to play.

'Of course, it wasn't really like that. But if I am to describe the breathtaking self-evidence with which she did anything to do with the instrument, I can find no better words than these: she picked it up and started to play. Just as if she had been waiting all that time for someone to bring her, at long last, the instrument for which she was born. "The girl emanates such *authority*," said Katharina Walther, when she saw her giving her first public performance at school. And that was exactly what Lea emanated when she picked up the violin: authority. Authority and grace.

'Where did it go, that natural authority that spoke out of all her playing movements? Where was it extinguished?'

Van Vliet choked on the smoke, his Adam's apple moved frantically. I looked at his face against the white wall: behind the healthy, sporty brown, a ruin came into view. With his sleeve he wiped the tears provoked by his coughing out of his eyes before going on.

'Something else happened to Lea: almost overnight a girl who had until now been so compliant turned into a little adult full of self-will. I experienced that transformation for the first time when we went in search of a violin teacher.

'For Lea there was only one woman in the picture, that was already clear the following morning. After school we drove to the three addresses that the conservatoire had given me. Lea roundly rejected the three women, and she always did it in the same way: no sooner had the conversation begun than she stood up without warning and walked silently to the door. I flinched every time, stammered words of apology and gestured ineffectually to express my helplessness. Afterwards, when I asked her in the street, I received no explanation by way of reply, only an obstinate shake of the head, accompanied by a defiant acceleration of her step. That was when I first sensed what it meant to have a daughter with a will of her own.

'MARIE PASTEUR. The name would become a guiding light for us both, which bathed everything in a brightness we had never known, and finally left ineradicable marks of burning. At the same time, it almost escaped me when, on the way home that day, we drove past the brass plaque on which it was engraved in gleaming black letters. Along with the words VIOLIN LESSONS. The house was at an intersection that I had already driven across when I became aware of what I had seen. I put my foot on the brake so violently that Lea shrieked and I was a hair's breadth away from causing a pile-up. I drove around the block and parked right in front of the house. The brass plaque hung on the cast-iron gate through which one entered the front garden, and now that the night was breaking, it was illuminated by the two light bulbs that seemed to float just above the gateposts.

'"Now let's try *this one*," I said to Lea and pointed at the name.

'As we crossed the front garden and walked towards the black door with the brass fittings, I saw in front of me Hans Lüthi, the biology teacher who was, after all, responsible for me sitting my school leaving exams. We had met in the basement of Francke's bookshop, where the books on chess were displayed. It was the morning of an ordinary week day, and I had bunked off Lüthi's class. I had pretended to be cocky and nonchalant, but I really felt awkward.

'"It's getting tight, Martijn," Lüthi had said, and looked at me with a calm, steady gaze. "I don't know if I can do anything else for you at the teachers' meeting."

'I shrugged casually and turned away.

'But his words had touched me. Not because they involved the threat of being thrown out of school, which I had seen coming for a long time, but because there had been grief in them, and concern for me, the rebellious, defiant boy who had been beyond school discipline for some time. Really and truly: there had been *concern* in his words and his expression. It was so long since anyone had been concerned about me that I was now practically distraught.

'Clutching the collected games of Capablanca, I stood gazing blankly at the shelf when Lüthi had touched me on the shoulder. "These are for you," he had said, and gave me two books. I don't think I said a single word of thanks, I was so surprised. Hans Lüthi, the man with the bourgeois name, the baggy corduroy trousers and the unkempt red hair, was already on his way upstairs by the time I understood what I was holding in my hands. It was two biographies, one of Louis Pasteur, the other of Marie Curie.

'They were to prove the most important books of my life. I devoured them, read them again and again. I didn't miss a single class in my last year of school and my science tests were flawless. Lüthi had hit the bullseye.

'I never found the words to tell him what he had done for me. I'm not good at that kind of thing.

'So now we were going to a woman whose name was Marie Pasteur. I was as excited as if I were on a first date when I rang the bell, the door sprang open and we walked up two flights of red-carpeted stairs.

'The woman waiting for us on the landing was wearing a flower-patterned apron and holding a wooden spoon, and looked at us with her eyebrows raised. I'm not easily intimidated, but Marie managed it, then and later. And even then I found only one way of dealing with her: I came straight out with it.

'"My daughter here,' I said, still on the stairs, "would like to take violin lessons with you."

'"You didn't even ask me," Lea said later. And Marie said I said it in a tone that said she *had* to go along with my wish; as if she had no choice but to accept Lea.

'She wasn't wild about our unexpected visit. She only let us in hesitantly, led us into the music room and then disappeared into the kitchen for a while. I could tell by the way Lea's eyes felt their way slowly, almost methodically, around the high, wide room that she liked it here. There was also the way she ran her hand caressingly over the many sofa cushions of smooth, shiny chintz. Then, when she got up and walked to the grand piano in the corner, I was sure that she wasn't going to disappear in silence again.

'It was no surprise that she liked the room. Furnished sparsely, but with exquisite taste, it was a place of silence. In some inexplicable way, the sounds of the street lost their power and insistence, and listened to each other as if they were only a distant echo of themselves. Ochre, beige and a light, diluted burgundy were the dominant colours, and after a while I noticed that in a vague, gentle way they stirred a memory of Loyola de Colón's frock coat. Gleaming parquet. An art nouveau candelabra. Big photographs of famous violinists on the walls. And chintz, a lot of chintz, a whole wall was covered with the smooth, seductive fabric.

She would love to bathe in chintz, Lea said after her first week's lesson.

'And then Marie Pasteur came into the room, the woman who would allow Lea's talent to unfold at an incredible, breathless, crazy rate; the woman with whom Lea could laugh, cry, rage and bubble over with joy as she could with no one else; the woman to whom my child would cling with a curious, absurd, life-endangering love; the woman I would fall in love with that very evening, without noticing; the woman to whom I brought an impossible love, for in her overflowing, reckless love Lea trusted no one but herself, and it was always completely clear that if I had allowed myself to be swept along in the wake of my own love it would have turned us into adversaries, even enemies, my daughter and I.

'All of that was still ahead of us when Marie came in. She was wearing an ankle-length batik dress, one of dozens that she owned; in my memory I always see her in one of those dresses, with soft leather slippers that were like a second skin. With her astonishingly small feet she walked in silence through the big rooms, and that was how it was on that evening too, when she walked obliquely across the room to us and sat down on the arm of a chair. One of her hands lay in her lap, with the other she supported herself on the back of the chair. The sight of her hands made me aware of my own hands: mine felt far too big and terribly ungainly in comparison to hers, which, as I would shortly see, combined slender elegance and great strength, a strength without the slightest trace of violence. When her hand rested in mine as we said goodbye,

I wished I could hold it for ever, so captivated was I by the strength of her handshake.

'Because that was what Marie Pasteur also emanated and what seemed to me on that first evening to constitute the whole of her being: an enormous strength without a trace of violence. It could also be discerned in her eyes, that strength, when she now turned her gaze on Lea and in a fleeting act of playful irony pursed her lips for a moment into a smile before asking a question of startling simplicity: "And why do you think the violin is the right instrument for you?"

'That was Marie. The woman who always sought clarity. Not the kind of clarity that I knew from science and also not the clarity of chess. A clarity that was harder to grasp and which I found weird in its intangibility. What she wanted to know was why people did what they did. Doesn't everyone want to know that? Yes, but Marie wanted to know *exactly* why they did it. And what it felt like. *Exactly* what it felt like. She wanted to know how it felt for her just as much as how it felt for the others; she was stubborn and unyielding when it came to understanding herself. So I came to know a passion which at first made everything – even the most familiar things – appear richer and more appealing, before at last plunging me into a darkness of incomprehension that I would never have encountered without Marie's idea of clarity.

'Lea didn't hesitate for a moment before answering Marie's question. "I feel it," she said simply, and there was something definitive in the few words that she uttered as naturally as breathing.

'"You feel it," Marie repeated hesitantly, slipping forward on the arm of the chair and linking her hands in her lap. A lock from her ash-blonde mane fell upon her forehead. She looked down at the shiny parquet floor. Her lips moved as if she were about to reapply her lipstick. At the time I had a sense that she didn't know how to continue the conversation. Later I discovered that it had been quite different: in a flash, the resolution in Lea's answer had prompted Marie's decision to take her on as a pupil. "I knew it was right; but it took me a few minutes to adjust to the idea. It would turn into something big and difficult, I sensed. And it would prove to be an unusually far-sighted decision on my part. I would rather have made it not at the end of a long day but in the morning." She smiled. "At about half past ten, perhaps?"

'"Would you like to play me something?" Lea asked into the silence, using the familiar *du*. I forgot to breathe. Admittedly she was still at an age when children call everyone *du*. But Lea was different. She had learned the difference between *du* and *Sie* at a very young age, she caused a great stir by doing so, and enjoyed it. But if she was angry with Cécile or with me, she addressed us as *vous*, and then it sounded as if we were in eighteenth-century French society. For example, if she happened not to like a dog, she would address it as *Sie*, and the bus would rock with laughter. So it was not a matter of chance, heedlessness or childish habit that Lea had addressed Marie as *du*.

'But even more than that familiar form of address, it was the question itself that alarmed me. It sounded, in fact, as if Lea were the teacher and Marie had to pass an exam. Of course, it could simply have been a clumsy choice of words and a lack of feel for nuance. But my mounting tension, which concerned both my feelings for Marie and my feelings for Lea, made me, it would turn out, clairvoyant. It made me sense something in Lea that would emerge more and more clearly over the coming years, without my ever finding the right word for it. It wasn't arrogance, it lacked the overbearing quality for that. Nor was it boastfulness or snootiness, Lea was too inconspicuous for that. Perhaps one might say that she exuded a terrible *demandingness* that seemed almost physical in its intensity, a demand that she made above all on herself, but which also cast a shadow on the others, who became smaller when it fell upon them.

'Above all that demand was made upon violin-playing, the holy mass of the bowed tones that she knew how to celebrate like a high priestess. It grew cooler when this priestess – as her competitors called her behind her back – entered a room. But the self-flagellating demand that gave her this aura of unapproachability and overload flourished beyond the music and poisoned so much else, above all the things on which Lea pounced in breathless, exalted eagerness, when she needed something new to fill the few breaks between practising and homework. She rapidly became an expert in tea, in porcelain, in old coins, and anyone who dared to step within the magic circle of her current theme became the victim of her lethal impatience, which was never expressed in harsh words, nor in words at all, but in the fact that her features, normally so vital, became angular and vague, until all that remained there was a smile of stony politeness.

'Eventually Marie would stand up against Lea's usurpation of her, which began that evening and knew no boundaries, none whatsoever. But at first she, who had no children, found the tyranny of an eight-year-old amusing, so she walked over to the grand piano on which lay her violin. From the pocket of her batik dress she took a black velvet ribbon and tied up her hair with it so that it didn't get in her way when she was playing. With a few brief strokes of the bow she checked that nothing needed tuning, and then Marie Pasteur, who had once set the Bern Conservatoire in uproar with her appearance and her sound, began to play a movement from a Bach sonata. *Johann Sebastian Bach*: she spoke the name as if it were the name of a saint.

'In the years that followed I heard a great deal of violin music. But nothing – or so says my memory, although I have learned to mistrust it more and more, with every year, with every pain – came close to what I heard that day. I'm sure Cécile would have said: *hallucinant*. And it would have been the right word, because Marie's playing had a clarity and precision, an intensity and depth that made everything, whatever else might have existed in the world of sounds, seem completely unreal. Loyola de Colón – how far in the past that was, and how imperfect it had been!

'Lea listened motionlessly, but her stillness now was something different from the trance in the railway station. She listened to the woman who would be her teacher, and she did it with the over-alert concentration with which for many years she would absorb every word that Marie said. I had no trouble copying that exclusive, consuming attention within myself. Not only was Marie Pasteur a beauty who could throw everything into total chaos; not only did she have that non-violent strength in her playing and her decisions; she could also play herself into a sacred passion that took your breath away. That was a reach for the stars, I thought, as my eye slid along the lines of her face. And those words flickered through my sleep: *reach for the stars*.

'When Marie had finished, Lea went to her and touched the violin as if it were a magical, metaphysical object. Marie ran her hand over her hair. "When does school finish on Monday?" she asked, and the time of her first lesson was established.

'And so began, soberly and unspectacularly, what would become a real explosion of talent, devotion and passionate will.

'I gave Marie my hand. "*Merci*" was all I could utter. "Yes," she replied, and her smile revealed that with that single word she was parodying my own taciturnity. Years later, shortly before the end, it was a few words more: "Thank you for bringing me Lea."'

These last words were swamped by tears. Van Vliet threw the cigarette away and clapped his hands in front of his face. His shoulders twitched.

'Come on, let's walk to the water,' he said then. I like to think about that sentence, and when in my thoughts I speak to the man in the photograph, raising his flask against the light, I call him *du* as well. Martijn, I say then, why didn't you phone me at least? If it really was the way I think it was.

But at the time I think we both thought the same thing. We were opening ourselves up to each other in a way which, as far as forms of address were concerned, called for a solid structure or at least some struts that would support whatever life had in store. Lest we fell into each other. So I addressed him by the formal *Sie*. Only once, much later, did he say *you*. And then it was like the last cry for help of a drowning man.

'That evening we forgot to eat,' Van Vliet continued by the water. 'We barely spoke, either. Lea scratched the strings with her bow and I sat at my desk and studied the photograph of Marie Curie.

'It bothered me that she looked bourgeois, compared with the elegance of Marie Pasteur. I didn't blame her. It was as if she were dumping me. Only her eyes survived the comparison. Admittedly, Madame Curie's eyes didn't have the gleam and the mercurial roguishness that made Marie Pasteur's green gaze so irresistible. On the other hand an unimaginable gentleness and kindness lay in the eyes of the only woman to have won two Nobel prizes for science. I had cut her photograph out of the book with which Hans Lüthi had ambushed and rescued me. Those eyes, which could have been the eyes of a nun, had long been my refuge when I was a student and didn't know how to go on, and was about to chuck it all in and flee to Alekhine, to Capablanca and Emanuel Lasker.

'*The sole secret of my success was my obstinacy.* This sentence doesn't come from Madame Curie, but from Louis Pasteur, although I attributed it to the great, nun-like researcher, because they were one and the same person in any case. Cécile had always been a bit jealous of her, and twice during our marriage the picture had fallen down and had to be reframed. Madame Curie had been allowed to study and Cécile hadn't. Admittedly, she was now in charge of training the nurses, and many young doctors sought her advice. But that did little to combat the bitter conviction that she, too, could have been a good doctor and researcher if her father hadn't gambled and drunk all the money away, so that she had to learn a profession as quickly as possible, and one that helped her to tend to her bedridden mother. In the darker times of our life together her bitterness also turned against me. "Fine, your parents were never there," she would say then, "but you have no idea how lucky that makes you."

'Lea was desperate because she couldn't hold the bow correctly, and stamped her foot with impatience. We tried together to remember the names of the violinists whose portraits hung in Marie's music room. Before I went to sleep I saw my daughter in front of me again, when Marie had challenged her to play something. I saw her demanding gaze and the way she had straightened with a pride that she had yet to earn. Then I thought back to the leaden gait and lowered eyes with which she had come out of school beside Caroline. Only two days had passed since then.'

7

VAN VLIET WAS sleeping when we drove back to Saint-Rémy. I was glad of that, since lots of trucks were coming towards us. Just before we drove into the town, when I had to brake sharply, he gave a start and rubbed his eyes. 'There's something I'd like to show you,' he said, and directed me to the clinic that had once been a monastery.

'Here,' he said, after we had walked through the park. 'This is where I stood with my binoculars, back then, and waited until she came out, into the garden, at about two or three. I simply couldn't bear it any more. I knew I couldn't visit her – the Maghrebi – but I needed at least to see her from a distance, so I got into the car in Bern and set off, often at night. I know the road by heart. I listened to Bach and . . . ' He sobbed. 'In the hotel they now greeted me like an old acquaintance. The first time I had made the mistake of saying something about Lea, and now they always welcomed me with, "*Ah, Léonie's father . . .* " It was torture.

'I destroyed my daughter's life with a violin. That was what I thought each time I drove away again. How often have I seen her sitting motionless on the wall over there, her arms wrapped around her knees; or running a hoe, hesitantly and aimlessly, along a furrow; once, too, standing still by the window of her room and looking out into the countryside, as if she were not of this world.

'But the worst picture was the one in which she ran the tip of her right index finger, bent slightly backwards, with her left thumb, it was a gentle, circling motion that she interrupted now and again to bring her finger to her lips and moisten it with the tip of her tongue. How often had I seen her make that motion when she was working on a piece with a lot of pizzicato! Her gaze had always been very concentrated, and even when she closed her eyes to moisten her finger, one sensed the attentiveness behind the closed lids, the attentiveness of a girl who was entirely focused on her task and completely absorbed in her craft. How different, how terribly different it was now! I had had to look for her for a long time and finally found her on a bench behind a woodpile. She was sitting there with her back bent, stroking her fingertip as she used to. Her gaze was lost. It came from nowhere and it went nowhere. She looked as if she were remembering the movement, perhaps even a spot that was sore from pressing down on the strings, but had forgotten what the reason for it was, and so, after a period of mechanical repetition, the movement became slower and more aimless, before finally ebbing away completely.

'After that the image of Lea's absent movement pursued me in everything I did. I couldn't help thinking about this scrap from her broken life. I thought: Where did your pride go, my child? Your confidence, which sometimes bordered on the blasé? The self-glorification of your merciless practising, which hardly allowed me to sleep? The insane longing to take the third step before the first and second? The crazy intention – hidden even from Marie – to play Paganini's capriccios before your twentieth birthday? Where did all that go? Why? Why don't you straighten up behind your bit of firewood, stretch your back, arch your eyebrows in critical amazement at the unsatisfactory achievements of other people and show them what a note is, a real note? Back then, on your first evening at Marie's, I was startled by the presumptuous undertone in your request – demand, in fact – to have something played for you, and even later a shiver sometimes ran down my spine when you allowed others to sense your superiority, your cool sublimity, which was nothing but exhaustion after the achievement of your self-defined, unreachable goals. I never told you: it sometimes wounded me, too, your impatience with imperfection, your over-hasty shake of the head, your boredom when you had to wait for the others, who were so much slower. When it got particularly bad, in my dreams afterwards I sat opposite you playing chess and ruthlessly allowed you to fall into a trap, only to wake up with a guilty conscience. It is good, and down to the wise prescience of our emotions, that you never really touched a chess piece. And none the less: I wish nothing more than that your features should reassemble into the face of my confident, impatient, frighteningly demanding daughter. I would a thousand times prefer even the most wounding expression to the lost gaze behind that damned stack of firewood.

'*Elle n'a pas pu avoir de jeunesse*, said the Maghrebi, and from his black gaze there emanated a reproach no less sombre than an accusation of murder. What is that supposed to mean? What does this man in the white coat know about you? Has he ever seen you coming back from Marie's, your cheeks feverishly hot? Or eating in the kitchen standing up so that you could get back to practising as soon as possible? Was he there in Geneva when the people stamped and whistled with enthusiasm? You were happy, I swear to you, even Caroline and her parents looked more and more concerned with each passing year when the topic of your success came up.

'*She wasn't allowed to be young*. It was pelting with rain the day he uttered that sentence, and afterwards I was drenched to the skin because I had spent hours on the beach kicking the same tin can in front of me so as not to choke on the words. Year after year I had tried in vain to persuade you at least to go on the merry-go-round on the day of Bern's Onion Market. "I'd rather practise," you said. *I'd rather practise*. Even today I hear you saying those words, and even today I hear the impatience and the quiet reproach in the voice that were supposed to indicate to me that I ought to know my unusual daughter and really should know better. Word for word, I would like to push that sentence into the dark gaze of the Maghrebi, to drive the accusation, the terrible accusation, that I had stolen your youth and thus preordained the path of your illness, back as far as possible into his eyes, further and further, until – right at the back, where thoughts are formed – it found itself in difficulties and, under the weight of the facts known to me alone, finally expired.

'The merry-go-round. Even the episode of the merry-go-round doesn't give the lie to what I say. No, even that is no burden to me. One day – it was spring and you were already thirteen – they were there again, the people with the merry-go-round, and suddenly you wanted a go. It was all about who could catch the many golden rings when they passed the stand on which the rings waited to slip forward and be pulled off. You were by far the oldest, and for one shameful second I thought it looked a little ridiculous, an already adult-looking young woman, amid fairground music and the shrieks of children, pursuing a childish pleasure from a missed past. Now once again you had red patches on your throat, and your expression was full of the hope and expectation of a five-year-old. And the golden ring came! Like a flash you pulled it off, and when the merry-go-round came to rest a few moments later, you ran to me with your eyes full of tears. I tried to decipher those tears and couldn't decide whether they were tears of joy over the golden ring or tears of grief over a missed childish happiness. You wiped those ambiguous tears away and set the ring on the palm of your hand. You knew you were supposed to give it back to the man with the cowboy hat. But you didn't care. "I'm going to give it to Marie," you said, and dragged me off with you. In the end Marie gave it back to you. It was the cruellest thing she could have done.'

A pack of tourists with cameras was passing as we got back into the car. Van Vliet snorted contemptuously.

'Van Gogh. You see his room here. Posthumous voyeurism. As if it wasn't enough that he had to live in this hole and cut off his ear. As if that *wasn't enough*!'

He gripped his shirt collar with both hands, pulled it open and drew it closed, so that his neck turned white, open and closed, again and again. I had been sorry that Tom Courtenay didn't punch the headmaster. Again and again I had been sorry, from the midday screening to the late show. I was really annoyed with him for not pulling that one off, really annoyed.

We stopped outside Van Vliet's hotel. He just sat there. In his thoughts he was still at the clinic.

'It started quite inconspicuously. An unsuitable word here, a skewed sentence there, a curious logic. Large gaps in between, so that you forgot it again. I was particularly taken aback by things like "Marie suffered from stage fright, she was so successful", "Zaugg wants to see the chalk for the high bar on my hands, she doesn't believe the rosin", and once I flinched so much that she noticed: "As a musician Niccolò was the best violinist because of that amazing reach." She always referred to Paganini by his first name, like a good friend.

'Then nothing particularly striking again for weeks. But I started taking notes. I hid my notebook right at the bottom of my desk, as if hiding it from myself. I was frightened, terribly frightened. But it was only ten years later that I started asking around among Cécile's circle if they'd also noticed anything skewed. Nothing distinct, all so long ago, they said.'

I said I wanted to go to my hotel to rest.

'But you'll come again?' It was a fearful expression, the expression of a boy who's afraid of the dark.

Yes, I said, I'd come back for dinner.

8

I LAY ON THE BED. I saw Van Vliet against the light. I saw him laughing. I saw him tugging at his shirt collar. I saw him with his binoculars on the clinic fence. When was the last time someone had moved me like this?

I thought of Cape Cod and Susan, my first wife, before Joanne. '*Adrian, is there anything that can upset you? Anything at all? Are you ever shaken?*' At the time I was working as a surgeon in A & E, with my hands in wounds and on shattered limbs from morning till night. You couldn't let it get to you, I said. Otherwise you'd be good for nothing. '*Yes, but it seems to leave your* soul *untouched.*' The morning after these words I got up early as if for an operation and at dawn I walked along the beach. The next night I slept on the sofa. You can't lie next to someone you think is a monster. We left the next morning. '*Hi*,' we said as we set off. In memory the word sounded bright and cruel, like a sound from a scalpel.

I went to sleep. When I woke up, the church tower was striking seven. It was dark. Leslie had phoned my mobile. I had left my watch in her bathroom.

'I know,' I said, 'but I actually didn't miss it.'

'You're sure you're OK?'

'No idea,' I said, 'no idea how I am.'

'Something's happened to you or is happening to you.'

'What was it like for you in boarding school? For you, I mean. How was it for you?'

'*Mon Dieu*, what am I supposed to say about that on the phone right now? I don't know . . . Sometimes I think I'm alone with the boy again, because . . . because . . . '

'Because we weren't a real family? Because you couldn't learn there? Is that what you think?'

'I don't know. That doesn't sound quite right. Oh, Dad, I don't know. It wasn't all that bad in the boarding school. You became independent. Only sometimes in the evening . . . Oh, *merde*.'

'Would you have liked to play an instrument?'

'You're asking some questions today! No idea. I don't think so. We aren't musical, are we?'

I laughed. 'Bye, Les. We'll talk again.'

'Yes, let's do that. Bye, Dad.'

Van Vliet waited in the empty hotel dining room. He had a carafe of red wine in front of him and a bottle of mineral water. He had drunk only water.

I told him about the conversation with Leslie.

'Boarding school,' he said. 'Lea and boarding school. That would . . . it would have been unthinkable.' Now he poured himself a glass of red wine and drank. 'Although . . . the Maghrebi . . . Perhaps in that case she wouldn't have ended up here. What do we really now about these things? *Merde*, what do we *know*?'

Now I ordered red wine as well. He grinned.

'Cécile's brother is dyslexic and has trouble with calculations. He doesn't understand the idea of quantity. It sounds crazy, but he just doesn't get it. It's called acalculia. Cécile could combat her fear that she might have passed the weakness on to Lea only by teaching her to read and do sums at the age of four. That was how Lea came to read Agatha Christie at six and was ahead of everyone in mental arithmetic. I had my doubts about whether we were doing it right, but I was also proud of my daughter, who learned so easily. The years of primary school were a walk in the park for her, there was never a conflict between homework and practising. I assume that Caroline, who sat next to her, copied down what was in her book when they were doing arithmetic. I also assume her parents knew that and that the glee with which they looked on when Lea stumbled later had its origins in that.

'Lea was soon the star of the school, flattered but also eyed with envy. As she often drove to Marie's immediately after class, the others saw her with the violin a lot, and that also reminded them of Lea's second life, of the fact that she refused to do gymnastics, something to do with the fact that it might endanger her hands. She didn't get on with Erika Zaugg, the teacher, whom she subjected to a devastating comparison with Marie; the woman made no secret of the fact that she thought Lea was petulant and simply hysterical. Things were quite different with the choleric male teacher, who was putty in her hands. I always listened out for alarming undertones when she talked about him or he about her, but he worshipped her from a considerable distance, and it was touching to see him riding roughshod over all the principles of justice and equal treatment when it came to Lea. She was, as I have said, a star, a real *vedette*.

'With the violin, too, it soon became apparent that she could become a star. In the first years of her work with Marie, Lea succeeded in every respect. From week to week the notes became purer and surer, the vibrato lost its initial jitter and became more regular, more tempered. In her many years of teaching, Marie had never had anyone who was at home with so many positions in such a short time, and Lea laughed till the tears came when I reminded her of how preoccupied she had been with the fact that Loyola de Colón had known exactly where to stop her hand sliding when switching positions. Double-stopping, the nightmare of all beginners, was difficult for Lea, too, of course. But constant practising soon gave her the necessary security, and the more difficult something was, the more of an obsession it became; it was very similar to me and chess.'

Van Vliet went to the toilet and when he came back we ordered something to eat. He mechanically ordered the same thing as me, his mind wasn't on it. Like before, when he had been alone by the water, the memory had taken him prisoner in the meantime, a memory that hurt.

'Scores,' he said. 'Lea read them as if they were the innate symbols of her spirit. I found it unbearable, no longer having access to this part of her, which was proving increasingly to be the most important. I needed to be able to read them as well. I asked if I could look over her shoulder when she was playing. She didn't say anything and started to play. After a few bars she stopped. "It's . . . it's not working, Dad," she said. There was a helpless testiness in the words. She was cross with me for putting her in the position of having to say that. I bought a second copy of the score and asked if I could sit on a chair in the corner while she played. She said nothing and looked at the ground. At Marie's there's also someone in the room when she plays, I thought. But exactly: *Marie* – and being with Marie was different from being with me; and with Marie *everything* was different from the way it was with me.

'I left the room and closed the door. It took quite a while before Lea started playing. I left the house and went to Krompholz, the music shop, where I bought a book about reading music for beginners. Katharina Walther looked at me with her intelligent, secretive expression. "There's nothing magical about it," she said, as I started flicking the pages. "Read it through and then read the notes along when she plays. In the next room, perhaps. She doesn't need to see." Incredible. She seemed to be able to read me – us – like a book.'

Van Vliet filled his glass and drained it in one gulp as if it were water. 'My God, why didn't I talk to her more often? And why didn't I listen to her later on when she warned me?'

He took out a ballpoint pen, opened his paper napkin, drew five lines and put some notes on them. 'Here,' he said, 'that's the beginning of Bach's Partita in E major. The notes that Loyola de Colón played in the station back then.' He gulped. 'And the last notes that Lea played before she sank into . . . her disturbed state.'

His fist closed slowly on the napkin and crushed those fateful notes. I topped up his glass. He drank and after a while he started talking again, calmly and clearly.

'I did as Katharina Walther suggested: I followed the score in the next room when Lea was playing. But it remained curiously strange to me, and it was a while before I understood why: I couldn't produce the related sounds. The notes remained without consequences for me. They were symbols that I could do nothing with and which, therefore, had nothing to do with me. So this part of Lea's mind remained closed to me, however hard I tried.

'One day when she was in school I went to her room, took the violin from its case, wedged it between shoulder and chin, put my fingers in position, as I had observed, and made the first stroke with the bow. Of course what came out was a lamentable sound, barely more than a scratch. But that wasn't what made me flinch. It was something I hadn't expected: a violent attack of guilty conscience, a kind of invisible spasm, and at the same time paralysing, accompanied by a feeling of impotence. Quickly and distractedly I put the violin back in its case and checked that everything was as it had been before. Then I sat down in the armchair in my room and waited for the thumping of my heart to subside. Outside dusk was beginning. It was dark when I understood at last: it had not been the usual guilty conscience that you get when you poke your nose into other people's affairs. It had been about something much more important and dangerous: by trying to imitate violin playing with my own body, I had crossed an invisible line that separated Lea's life from mine, and had to separate it so that it could be entirely *hers*. There had also been a hint of that feeling, I thought now, in the testiness with which Lea explained to me that she didn't want me looking over her shoulder when she played. And now I remembered how the eight-year-old girl had resisted me after Loyola's playing, in the station back then, when I wanted to pull her to me as usual.

'And Marie? I thought. With her that line didn't exist. On the contrary, in her playing and otherwise Lea was trying to be like Marie. Was there another line that I just couldn't see?'

Van Vliet looked at me. It wasn't clear whether he was hoping for an answer – the insight of an outsider, perhaps – or whether he was only seeing my view as someone who wanted his hardship and insecurity to be recognized and accepted. I touched his arm – who knows why? Who knows if it was a suitable gesture, a gesture corresponding to his fragility. He had left his burning cigarette in the ashtray and was lighting a new one. I looked past him at the big mirror on the wall that showed us both. Two illiterates in the field of proximity and distance, I thought, two illiterates in the field of familiarity and strangeness.

'When Lea came through the door that evening,' Van Vliet continued, 'she was standing in front of me again: as someone who wasn't just *able* to do something that I would never be able to do, but someone who *was* something that I would never be: a musician whose life consisted increasingly of scores and notes. "What is it? What's up?" she asked. "Nothing," I said. "It's nothing. Shall I cook something?" But she was already at the fridge, bit into a cold sausage and grabbed a piece of bread. "Thanks, but I'd rather do a bit more practising." She disappeared into her room and closed the door.

'I could only contribute one thing: I explained the physics of recorder notes to her. She was addicted to their glassy tone and her attempt to make it, after touching it for the first time.

'In terms of technical problems there was only one with which she had to struggle until the end: trills. They often didn't have the silken lightness and above all the metronomic regularity that they should have had. Particularly when they lasted for a long time, fatigue and forced, defiant-sounding thrusts crept in, creating an impression of effort and over-exertion. Lea furiously massaged her cramped fingers, held them in warm water and kneaded a ball to strengthen them while watching television.

'But my daughter was happy. In love with the violin, in love with the music, in love with her talent and, yes, in love with Marie.

'"*Amoureuse?*" The dark hand of the Maghrebi with the silver pen paused abruptly. "*Ouais,*" I said and did everything I could to make the word sound as vulgar as it would have sounded, in my imagination, coming from a delinquent who was receiving a ruthless going-over from a police inspector in court. I even crossed my legs like a snotty little gangster who's enjoying his last scrap of freedom, which consists in not giving the inspector a single word.

'"*Vous voulez dire . . .*"

'"*Non,*" I replied, and it was more a yapping snap than an articulate denial. The doctor darted his nib back and forth, the sound was very loud, louder than the hum and hiss of the fan. It took him some time to get his irritation under control.

'"*Alors, c'était quoi, cette rélation?*"

'How could I have explained it to him? How could I explain it to *anyone*?

'Marie, I'm sure, had a description for her relationship with Lea. But I never asked her. And, in fact, I didn't *want* to know. I know what I saw and heard, and I don't know if there's anything to know beyond that. Marie could not be criticized, I grasped that quickly. It was better not to ask about Marie. It was out of the question not to listen with complete concentration when Marie was being discussed. Disbelief appeared on Lea's face whenever I forgot something to do with Marie, even something quite trivial. It was annoying for her when someone else had the audacity to be called Marie. It was unimaginable that Marie could become ill. It was out of the question that she should ever take a holiday. Every day

I waited for Lea to want a batik dress and chintz cushions. But things between them weren't actually so simple.

'Generally speaking, it wasn't as I had imagined. When I sometimes stood in front of Marie's house on late winter afternoons and watched the shadow play that Marie and Lea put on behind the curtains, I felt excluded and envied them both the cocoon of sounds, words and gestures that they seemed to have spun for themselves, and in which there was none of the friction and irritability that increasingly appeared in the institute, since I had made it clear with very few words that from now on it would be Lea first of all, then Lea again, and only then the lab.

'At the very beginning I made the mistake of ringing on Marie's door. It was the last five minutes of the lesson, which I sat and listened to. I have never been so much in the way as I was then. Marie and Lea left the music room, not furious, not reproachful, only very determined, completely preoccupied with one another and without a backward glance; as if there was only empty space there. There must have been a perfect harmony between the two of them, I thought for almost two years, and there were moments of fierce jealousy in which I didn't know which hurt more: Marie taking Lea away from me or Lea erecting a boundary in front of Marie which I would never be able to overcome.

'That was how it was until the day when Lea was supposed to seek out the three-quarter size violin from Krompholz. Katharina Walther wasn't exactly over the moon that Marie was there too. "Marie Pasteur. Yes, yes, Marie Pasteur," she said when I next visited the shop. Apart from that I was never able to entice a word out of her. I didn't like those words. There was something omniscient and almost papal about them, and that day I was no longer sure if I liked her severe hairdo with the bun at the back. Now, however, she was acting correctly, too correctly, in fact, with her glances as well as with her words. No meddling, no complicity, nothing.

'Lea tried out the three violins in turn. How grown-up and professional she looked in comparison with our first visit here! When the first round was over, the process of negative selection began. The first one went quickly. Lea exchanged a glance with Marie, but it wouldn't have been necessary, we all heard it. The second one sounded good, but no comparison with the third. "Astonishing for an instrument of this size," said Marie. It was impossible that Lea didn't hear it too, and in response to the tone, which was so much better than that of her previous instrument, her face had begun to light up. But now she picked up the second one again and played for a few minutes. Marie leaned against the counter, her arms folded. When I replayed the scene in my mind later on, I was sure that she knew what was going to happen. "I'll take this one," Lea said.

'Katharina Walther's lips parted as if she wanted to protest, but she said nothing. After a few seconds staring at the floor, still holding the violin, Lea raised her head and looked challengingly at Marie. I knew that look, and I didn't know it. She could be contrary and headstrong, Cécile and I had encountered that often enough. But this was Marie, uncriticizable Marie, standing here. And it hurt Marie Pasteur. It hurt her so much that she mechanically twisted her bracelet and swallowed once too many times.

'The next day Lea went to Krompholz on her own and swapped the second violin for the third. She didn't say much, Katharina Walther told me. Contrite? No, Lea hadn't actually seemed that way, she said; more disturbed. She hesitated. "By herself," she added.

'A few days later eczema broke out and gave us the worst three weeks since Cécile's death. It started with Lea's fingertips getting hot. Every few minutes she went to the bathroom and held them under cold water, and that night I didn't get a wink of sleep because I constantly heard water running. In the morning she sat on the edge of the bed and pointed, wide-eyed, at her skin, which was starting to discolour and harden. She stayed at home and I cancelled my participation at a conference. Afterwards I spent hours on the phone to former fellow-students who had become doctors, until at last I got an appointment with one who knew about skin. He studied and palpated Lea's skin, which was becoming greyer by the hour and was now starting to itch. Eczema, caused by an allergy. Violin? Then it could be the rosin, he told me. Terror flooded my limbs as if I had been diagnosed with cancer. Lea loved the dark brown resin that had a golden sheen when you held it to the light. At first she had even secretly licked it. Was this the end? A violinist with an allergy to rosin? Wasn't that impossible?

'With a fanaticism that I'm uncomfortable looking back on, I studied the literature on allergies and found out how little is known. Mountains of ointments piled up in the bathroom. My daily phone conversation with the doctor prompted mockery from the assistants, I could tell from their incautious giggling. The pharmacist raised her eyebrows in astonishment when I appeared for the third time. When she talked about stress, psychosomatic illness and homeopathy I switched pharmacies. I believe in cells, mechanisms and chemicals, not in subtle fairy stories delivered with a knowing expression.

'Ruthlessly and in great detail I forced Lea to remember everything she had come into contact with over the past few days, particularly anything unusual. I even wanted her to remember smells. My relentless probing led to tears.

'And then, all of a sudden, she got it: the benches in the classroom suddenly had a different smell. We went to school and talked to the janitor. And, sure enough, he had been using a new cleaning material. I took a sample and the doctor did an allergy test. It was this cleaning material, not the rosin. I noted its chemical composition and stuck the piece of paper to the fridge. It hung there until it turned yellow.

'I wanted to celebrate this redeeming news and we went out to an expensive restaurant. But Lea crouched over her plate and rubbed her raw, unfeeling fingertips over the tablecloth. Even today I think I can hear the quietly abrasive sound.

'For a week it was as if she were wearing gloves made of sandpaper. She picked up the violin several times a day, but it was hopeless. Then the skin crust began to burst and the new skin beneath it appeared, with a red pulse under it, and which could not endure any kind of contact. When the diseased skin finally fell off like a collection of exploded thimbles, Lea ran through the flat, calming her sensitive fingertips by blowing on them and every hour she tested whether they could now bear contact with a string. For days, it seems to me now, we lived as though in a prison whose invisible walls were formed by fear anticipated for all eternity, and something like that could happen at any time.

'And there was another prison cell: the lessons with Marie were cancelled. In a choking voice, in which fury and tears mixed together, Lea told me that someone else – someone *else*! – was with Marie in the music room at her times – *her times*! At last, when I dropped her off at Marie's, I saw that her hands, with their unnaturally red fingertips, were drenched in sweat and her throat was covered with red patches of agitation.

'The Maghrebi wanted to know if anything else had happened to Lea's hands. The question caught my attention, I can't deny it. No, I said. For a while he said nothing and the noise of the fan became really insistent. No, I said again, against my will. I didn't mention the business with the merry-go-round and the gold ring either.

'My colleagues were angry with me for not going to the conference because of Lea's eczema – because of *eczema*! – to present our latest research results. And above all the fact that I had cancelled without sending Ruth Adamek in my place. "Could it be that you've *forgotten* again?" she asked, and there was a harshness in her voice that showed me that I was losing more and more ground.

'The senior echelons of the university were disappointed, too. But there was no real apparent danger. As long as I didn't steal the silver spoons they couldn't touch me. And at the time I couldn't have known about the disturbing events that would lead me to steal them.'

9

'LEA'S FIRST PUBLIC PERFORMANCE took place on the day when the Year Four primary school children left school. The headmaster, a curmudgeonly, feared man, had invited her into his office, the secretary had offered her tea and biscuits, and then he had asked her if she would play something that day. She must have been so flattered that she agreed on the spot. Excited, almost feverish, she burst in on a meeting in my office. I walked up and down with her in the corridor until her flickering panic had settled. Then I sent her to Marie and by the time she came home she knew what she was going to play.

'I had barely known stage fright until then. Before my own lectures I had been psyched up rather than jittery, and the first time I found myself standing in an auditorium and found the spatial arrangement, which I had experienced from the other side over many years as a student, more ridiculous than frightening. But now that it was no longer about me, I was to become acquainted with stage fright.

'I learned to hate and fear it, and I also learned to love it and to miss it when it was over. It united Lea and me, and it also divided us. Her moist hands became my moist hands, her distractedness and agitation filled me too. There were moments when our nerves vibrated like those of a single creature. Indeed, it couldn't have been otherwise; Lea fell into an abyss of abandonment if she thought I didn't share her feverish excitement. And yet she also insisted that *she* was the one who had reasons to be afraid, not me. She didn't insist with words; we barely spoke about the omnipresent, feverish delusion that enveloped us. But she immediately left the room again when she encountered me smoking one of my rare cigarettes at the balcony window. In spite of everything, she's still a little girl, I would say to myself, what do you expect?

'At such moments I felt the loneliness that Cécile had left in me. I felt it like an inner frost.

'When Lea came out of the bathroom on the evening of the concert, it took my breath away. This wasn't a little girl of eleven. This was a young lady waiting for the spotlights to come on. We had chosen the plain black dress together. But where had she learned to powder and comb herself like that? Where had she got that lipstick? She enjoyed my perplexity. I took a photograph of her, which I put in my briefcase and never again swapped for another one.

'Why isn't it possible to stop time? Why couldn't things have stayed as they were one sultry stormy evening in high summer, an hour before Lea was carried away by all those eyes on her and those clapping hands, stolen right in front of my eyes, while I was unable to do the slightest thing about it?

'But I have no coherent memory of that evening. It's as if the violence of emotions had torn it into pieces, leaving only scattered fragments. We took a taxi to school; this evening the traffic must not get in our way. As we drove past the station I thought: It's been less than three years and now she's giving her first concert. I don't know if that was Lea's thought as well, but she put her hand in mine. It was damp and didn't feel like a hand that would soon be playing Bach and Mozart with confident fingers. When I felt her head on my shoulder, I thought for a moment that she was about to turn round. It was a redeeming thought that flashed into my mind in the restless sleep of the coming night, accompanied by a feeling of impotence and futility.

'The next thing I see in front of me is Marie Pasteur pressing the cross on Lea's forehead with her thumb. I couldn't believe my eyes and lost my composure completely when Lea crossed herself. Lea had never been baptized and had, as far as I knew, never held a Bible in her hand. And now she was crossing herself, with a natural grace that suggested she had been doing it all her life. It took a long time before I understood that it wasn't what it had seemed at first, Marie's attempt to turn Lea into a Catholic. It was simply a ritual that connected them, a gesture with which they reassured each other of their affection and their bond, which seemed greater than they themselves were. And even when I had understood at last, I was left with a quiet sensation of alienation and betrayal. That evening the vision flickered into my mind again and again, before being overlaid by events on the stage of the hall.

'Lea climbed the few steps, her hand on her dress so as not to trip over the hem. In the middle of the stage, a few steps away from the grand piano, she stopped and bowed several times to the applauding audience. I had never seen that before. I watched her dainty movements with fascination. Had Marie shown her that? Or did she simply have it within her?

'Marie gave her time. It was to be Lea and Lea alone who was standing in the spotlight. She was wearing a midnight-blue dress with a high neck, and because she had also worn batik at our first meeting, for a moment I felt as if they had both brought the music room from Marie's flat with them. It was a beautiful feeling, because it meant that Lea was protected by Marie on stage just as much as she was when she practised in her flat. But it was fleeting, that feeling, and soon it was wiped away by another: that up there, in spite of Marie, Lea was all alone with her violin and her gift – a girl who, for all her ladylike appearance and behaviour, had been in the world only for eleven years, and whom nobody would be able to help if she stumbled.

'I have spoken at many conferences in front of many very important people, and at chess tournaments I have sat on a stage and had to fend entirely for myself. But that was nothing in comparison with the task of enduring Lea's loneliness up on that stage. Particularly in the seconds before she started playing. Marie gave the chamber pitch, Lea tuned to it, a small pause, then she corrected the tension of her bow, another pause to wipe her hand on her dress, the glance at Marie, the lifting of the bow, and then at last she started playing Bach's music.

'At that very moment I wondered whether her memory was adequate to the task at hand. There was nothing, not the slightest point of reference to argue against it. Memory had never been an issue. I had seen it as the most natural thing in the world that Lea knew certain pieces by heart. It had seemed as natural to me as my ability to keep whole games of chess in my head and play them blind. So where did this sudden doubt come from?

'I no longer remember the music, the memory is mute and filled entirely with the fearful admiration with which I followed the energetic movements of Lea's arm and her sure, nimble fingering, copied from Marie's fingering, as I remembered it from the first evening. I had seen it all a thousand times, and yet now it seemed, as all those strange eyes watched, different, more admirable and mysterious than usual. It was Lea, my daughter, playing up there!

'Noisy applause. Delicate Markus Gerber clapped for longest. His face glowed. He had dressed as if he were the one who had to go on stage. Sometimes Lea was indulgent, sometimes irritated, when he wanted to walk her to school. I felt for him; soon she would drop him.

'Marie stayed seated at the grand piano. Lea bowed. Later, when I was lying awake, I was troubled by something that was hard to grasp. She had bowed as if she *agreed* with this applause. As if the world simply *had* to cheer her. That had bothered – or rather – disturbed me more than I was able to admit. It wasn't (as I thought at first) because it contained vanity and presumption. No, it was the reverse: her posture, her movements and her expression expressed a message of which she knew nothing as yet, and in a certain sense would never know anything until the end: that she must never be left alone with the thing that she was able to do, the thing she worked on with such boundless devotion; that others must on no account be allowed to encounter her playing heedlessly; that it would a disaster if the listeners withdrew their love and admiration. In retrospect, I know: what I saw there on the stage and what I felt to be something ominous was a harbinger, a harbinger of all the dramas that were yet to come, once she had taken the first step into the public view that evening.

'The second piece was a Mozart rondo. And that was when it happened: Lea played a phrase too many and the motif that comes up most frequently crept in where it didn't belong. It was quite a natural mistake that no one would have noticed had it not been for the piano accompaniment replacing the orchestra originally envisaged by Mozart. Marie and Lea's notes no longer matched, and dissonance and rhythmic chaos ensued. Marie took her hands off the keys and looked over at Lea, her eyes large and dark. Was it dismay that lay in those eyes? Or reproach? The reproach at betraying the perfection she was trying to guide Lea towards, hour for hour, week for week?

'I didn't like those eyes. Until now my gaze had drifted quite often to Marie. I liked the way she sat there in her dark, mysterious dress, her strong, slender hands on the keys, her face full of concentration on their concerted playing. As so often I imagined what it would be like with her, with her on her own, in a world without Lea – just to return with a lacerating feeling of betrayal to the reality where my little daughter, my big daughter, was having her debut, in a school hall, but still. Now, however, I was repelled by Marie's eyes, in which I read a nonsensical accusation, an accusation fired at an eleven-year-old girl who had made a mistake in a piece of music. Or perhaps it was not an accusation. Was Marie simply confused and, behind her dark gaze, seeking a possible way of finding her way back into Lea's playing? Lea herself had – after a fearful and helpless glance at Marie – carried on with the superfluous phrase, yes, that's the right word: *carried on*, the way one carries on even though there's no longer any point – just because stopping would be even worse. During the night I thought: No, I never want to see my daughter carrying on like that. Again and again I thought this thought, the whole night, and it kept coming back later, right to the end, and even today it sometimes ambushes me, a useless, phantom thought from a lost time.

'Suddenly Marie seemed to understand what had happened, there were a few hesitant, still-inappropriate notes and then harmony was re-established and maintained until the end. Lea's playing of the rest was clean and error-free, but there was a flatness to her notes, as if carrying on without Marie as she had just done had used up all of her strength. Perhaps it was my imagination. Who knows?

'The applause was noisier than it had been after the first piece, some people even stamped and whistled appreciatively. I listened hard: was that forced, dutiful applause? Was it so strong and sustained to console Lea and to say to her: it doesn't matter, you were good anyway? Or were those little boys and girls so natural and uninhibited in their judgement that Lea's oversight simply had no meaning for them at all?

'Lea bowed, more hesitantly and stiffly than after the first piece, and then she tried to catch my eye. How do you meet the insecure, apologetic gaze of an eleven-year-old daughter who has just had her first misfortune? I put into my own expression everything I could in terms of confidence, generous trust and pride in her. With eyes that were starting to sting, I probed her face: did she understand what had happened? How was she dealing with it? Did those twitching eyelids mean that she was battling against her disappointment and self-directed rage? Then Marie came and stood next to Lea and put her arm around her shoulder. Now I liked her again.

'Lea had played by heart, even though she had the score. Contrary to her habits, she set the book down on the kitchen table when we came home. On the way she hadn't said a word. I thought about how stiffly she had stood there when

Marie had stroked her hair to say goodbye, so I was careful not to touch her. It was the first time I had encountered my daughter in a state that I would learn to fear: as if at the slightest touch, even if it was only words, she would shatter.'

Van Vliet paused, his eye sliding diagonally downwards and seeming to penetrate every object with a kind of searing emptiness.

'In the end she really did shatter, she shattered into a thousand pieces.'

He took great gulps. A trickle of red wine ran from the corner of his mouth and dripped on his shirt collar. 'I studied the score of Mozart's Rondo on the kitchen table, all night. Köchel 373. I will never forget that number; it's as if it's etched into me. I found two passages that might be responsible for the mistake, the superfluous phrase. I didn't dare to ask. I put the score on the chest of drawers in the corridor where Lea sometimes set her scores down when she came home. She left it there. As if it didn't exist. In the end I discarded it. It was the only score that I threw away when I moved into the little flat.

'This event represented a first hair crack in Lea's confidence. It was weeks before we could talk about it. And then she told me: she had had to struggle to resist an impulse to hurl the violin into the audience. I was much more startled by that than by her slip. Wasn't what was happening to my daughter much too dangerous? Wasn't the ambition that Marie had unleashed in her like a fire that could no longer be extinguished?'

10

'WE TOOK the night train to Rome. Lea had always been amazed by trains with sleeping carriages. The idea that there were trains with beds in, which you lay down upon only to wake up somewhere entirely different – it seemed to her like some kind of magic. Allowing her to experience that same magic in her own body was the only way I could think of to overcome the paralysis into which she had fallen after her mistake in the Rondo. For the first few days she had stayed in bed and drawn the curtains like a seriously ill patient. She didn't even want to talk to Marie when she called. The violin case stood banished behind the cupboard.

'I had expected something, but nothing so violent. She had had that noisy applause, after all, even Caroline's parents had clapped. The headmaster had come out on stage and attempted to kiss her hand, failing grotesquely. But Lea's face was increasingly frozen and had assumed a mask-like immobility. I stared sleeplessly into the darkness and tried to banish the image of that lifeless, bitter face. In the eleven years since I had known this face, it had not seemed strange to me for a second, and I wouldn't have considered it possible that it might one day become so. Now that it was happening, for a moment I lost the ground under my feet.

'Her face was back to normal when we sat over breakfast in the dining car. And the deeper we travelled into the flickering Italian high summer, allowing ourselves to be captivated by the buildings, the piazzas and the sea, the more the traces of exhaustion left on her face by tireless practising faded away. Lea already looked quite grown-up, I thought, and there were appreciative whistles for her appearance. We never once talked about music and the Rondo.

'At first I said the occasional sentence about Marie, but my words went unanswered, as if they had not been uttered. If we passed a postcard stand I hoped Lea would buy one for Marie. But nothing happened.

'Sometimes she would forget something. It was just small things that didn't matter: the name of our hotel, the number of the bus line, the name of a drink. I thought nothing of it. Nothing that stuck. It was wonderfully hot and Bern with Ruth Adamek was wonderfully far away.

'The church the sounds were coming from was on a small, idyllic square. The church door was open; people sat outside on the steps, listening. Lea recognized the piece before I did: it was the music by Bach that Marie had played on the evening of our first meeting. It wasn't a spasm that ran through her body, more a kind of stiffening, a lightning-quick build-up of tension. She left me standing there and disappeared into the church.

'I sat down outside. My thoughts returned to the moment when I had seen the brass plaque with Marie Pasteur's name as I drove by. I wished I hadn't seen it. It could have happened so easily, I thought: a car that had distracted me, a blinking neon light, a striking passer-by – and the plaque would never have entered my field of vision. Then Lea wouldn't have left me standing there.

'As she came back out her face was twitching, and when she sat down next to me it came spilling out of her: the fear of having disappointed Marie; the fear of losing her affection; the fear of her next appearance. I stood up for Marie and slowly the tears ebbed away. She bought a dozen postcards, we went in search of stamps, and that same evening she threw three cards to Marie into the postbox. She tried to call to announce the cards, but there was no one at home. I booked a flight for the next day and after landing in Zurich I rang Marie. At home Lea took her violin out from behind the cupboard and went to her first lesson for three weeks. She played for half the night. The fever had returned.'

We were standing in the hotel corridor, by the lift. 'Good night,' I had said, and Van Vliet had nodded. The lift door opened. Van Vliet went and stood by the light barrier. I waited as he searched for words.

'There I sat in that hall back then, listening to the thing that had become the most important thing in my life: Lea's playing. The first performance, upon which, I sensed, so much depended. And just then my imagination breaks out and seeks a world without Lea, a world with only Marie. Do you know that one too: the imagination wandering off at the crucial moment and going its own uncontrollable ways, which reveal that you are still quite a different person from the one you thought you were? Precisely then, when anything can happen in the soul except that one thing: betrayal by one's own wayward imagination?'

11

SOMERSET MAUGHAM couldn't hold my attention. I set the book down, opened the window and listened to the darkness of the night. I hadn't had an answer to Van Vliet's question. He had tilted his head to one side and looked at me from half-closed eyes, ironic, complicit and sad. Then he had stepped out of the light barrier and the lift door had closed. Was it just that the question was so unexpected? Or was it the startling intimacy that had taken my language away, an intimacy that went far beyond my having become his audience?

Liliane. Liliane, who had dabbed the sweat from my brow when I was operating. Liliane, who always knew which intervention I was going to make next, which instrument I was going to need. Liliane, whose thoughts hurried so far ahead that words were not necessary and we worked together in mute harmony. Two, three months had passed like that. Her bright, blue gaze above the mask, her swift, calm hands, *grand*, her Irish accent, nods in the corridor, the clatter of her clogs, my unnecessary glance into the nurses' room, the cigarette between her full lips, her ironic gaze in response, longer than necessary, one single visit to the boss's room, that always surprising word *grand*, as I had heard it in Dublin, a moment too long by the door as she left, that movement of her hips, unconscious, unnoticeable, a gentle, silent closing of the door, which was like a hope and a promise.

And then the emergency operation on the night of Leslie's birth. First the exhausted face of Joanne, the sweat-slicked hair, Leslie's first cry. Afterwards at home by the open window, the snowy air of Boston, uncertain sensations, now things were irreversible. Dozing instead of proper sleep. Then the call from casualty. Five hours with Liliane's blue eyes above the mask. I don't know if it was by chance that she was standing by the exit when I left, I never asked her. I can't walk through the early morning light without remembering how we went together to her flat, which to my surprise was only two streets away from ours. We walked in silence, swapping glances every now and again. I hoped she would take my arm, instead her childish skipping, up on to the pavement, down from the pavement, her apologetic, challenging smile, one tooth slightly paler than the others in the lamplight. When we sat on the steps in front of her house, she edged closer and rested her head on my shoulder. It might have been shared exhaustion and shared contentment about the successful outcome of the operation. It could also have been more. Our white, melting breath. 'I make good shakes,' she said quietly. 'In fact I make the best shakes in town. My strawberry shakes are particularly legendary.' The shared laugh, the common shaking of our bodies. I stopped on the stairs and closed my eyes, my hands clenched in my coat pockets. Her voice came from above: 'My shakes are particularly good.'

There was something of the stray cat about her, sitting there on the sofa, her legs underneath her, her bright hair loose, the huge mug with the straw at her lips. She emanated something free and inconstant, something very different from Joanne's determination and diligence, which would later make her a successful businesswoman. What lay in her unimaginably concentrated blue eyes? Was it devotion? Yes, that was the word: *Devotion*. From that devotion flowed her concentrated movements at work, her anticipation of the things that I would need next, and I also saw devotion when our eyes met above the mask. *I cannot be awake, for nothing looks to me as it did before, / Or else I am awake for the first time, and all before has been / a mean sleep*. She knew a lot of Walt Whitman off by heart, and I forgot space and time when she recited it with eyes closed, smoke in her voice, melancholy and, yes, devotion. I longed for that devotion as it grew light behind the curtains and trucks thundered past more and more frequently on the nearby motorway. In the middle of that longing, bright panic exploded in me. I saw Joanne's sticky hair, *Thank God it's over*, and I heard Leslie's cry.

Liliane's devotion: I feared it as one can only fear oneself. I sensed that she would be something quite unlike anything I had experienced before, with Susan, Joanne and a few other fleeting acquaintances. That I would sink into her and disappear, waking up again somewhere else, far from Joanne and Leslie and, yes, far from myself – or far from the me that I had known until now.

I have never sensed so precisely what it is: the strength of will, as I opened my eyes, looked at Liliane and said: *I have to leave. It's . . . I just have to.* Her gaze faltered; the twitch in her mouth was that of someone who knew that she was about to lose, and who, now that it was clearly happening, was torn in two even so.

We stood in the corridor and rested our foreheads together, our eyes closed, hands clasped behind each other's necks. I felt as if we could each gaze through each other's forehead as if into a tunnel of thoughts, fantasies and expectations, a long tunnel of our possible impossible future; we looked into the tunnel as we imagined it; it was the tunnel of the other and at the same time our own, the two conjoined and merged; we went all the way down that tunnel to the back, where it was lost in vagueness, our breath harmonized, the temptation of lips, we experienced, penetrated, burned our life together, which wasn't possible because it wasn't possible for me.

For another week Liliane went on wiping the sweat from my brow. Then, one Monday morning, my secretary brought me an envelope, hesitantly, because she knew that it was from Liliane. A little sheet of paper, actually just a note, bright yellow: *Adrian – I tried, I tried hard, but I can't, I just can't. Love. Liliane.*

I don't have a photograph of her and the three decades have blurred her features. But two precise memories have remained, less in their sensual contours and in their emanation: at the table in the nurses' room, smoking, and on the sofa, her legs beneath her, the straw between her lips. And I took a photograph of the steps on which we sat back then, in the early morning light, outside her house. Before we left Boston I went there and took the picture. It had snowed all night, and snow was piled up on the railings and the steps. A picture from a fairy tale. I think of it on Leslie's birthday, always. The fact that I was a hair's breadth away from betraying her that day.

A year later Liliane rang me at the clinic. She had fled Boston and gone to Paris, to Médecins sans Frontières. Missions in Africa and India. It gave me a pang. I could have imagined doing the same thing. On the night after the call, I claimed I was on night shift and stayed in the clinic. It suited her so well, so incredibly well, and I envied her the consistency of her inconstant life, the consistency with which I imagined her. *Faces along the bar / Cling to their average day: / The lights must never go out, / The music must always play* . . . She had also recited those lines from W. H. Auden back then, on the sofa. They had sounded like something merely atmospheric, something private, like a tune accompanying a painting by Edward Hopper. Only later did I discover that they were part of an eminently political poem about the German invasion of Poland. And that had suited her, too: in her blue gaze, apart from devotion there had also been fury, fury about the cowards and evil-doers in this world, and so she had put her quick, calm hands and the speed of her thought at the service of their victims.

Other calls came at irregular intervals, they were strange conversations, quick and intense, *grand*, she spoke about hunger and other sufferings, then again she described her mood to me, as if in that corridor back then we had touched not just foreheads but lips. I told her the name of the clinic where I would be working in Switzerland, and calls arrived there as well. When she told me about Médecins sans Frontières, afterwards I had had the feeling of living on the wrong continent. And when we landed at Kloten Airport I thought: Now I'm closer to her. It was nonsense, because she could have been anywhere; but I thought it anyway. I was startled and darted a furtive glance at Leslie beside me. When the calls stopped years later, I called Paris one day and asked for her. She had died in an accident on one of her missions. At that point it became clear to me that I had been leading a life with her all that time. The months in which we had heard nothing from each other, and in which I hadn't thought expressly about her, changed nothing about that. Our life together went on, silent, uninterrupted and secret.

Van Vliet's question in front of the open lift had stripped me of my composure, because it had made it clear to me that I was still living that silent life with Liliane, even though there was no one left for me to keep it secret from. *Un accident mortel*, the Frenchman had said on the telephone. Something within me must have refused to accept it, so I carried on with her as if she were still living her wayward life, her life and my life and our life.

I thought about Joanne's farewell, that final farewell at the airport. *I will say one thing for you, Adrian. You are a loyal man, a truly loyal man.*' I don't know why, but it sounded as if she were identifying a character defect that had caused her to suffer. A little as if she had said: a man without imagination, a bore. I had planned to stand on the viewing platform and watch the woman I had been married to for eleven years flying back to her home. But her observation had disturbed me and I decided not to. At home I looked for the photograph of Liliane's house with the snowy steps.

I had gone to sleep in my clothes and I was freezing. Just before I woke up, I saw Liliane walking down the clinic corridor in her clogs. She was now dressed in batik and bathing in chintz.

I showered, changed my clothes and walked through Saint-Rémy at dawn. I stood outside Van Vliet's hotel for a while. I took a few photographs and then slept for a little longer until it was time to collect him.

12

THE LANDSCAPE of Provence was bathed in shadowless, chalky winter light as we set off. Each section looked like an enormous watercolour in hues that seemed as if they'd been mixed with white. I saw in front of me the heat-shimmering, endless roads on which I had driven through the American West with Joanne and Leslie. *Changing skies*, a formulation that I had always liked because it expresses in two words the experience of the vast dimensions that are such a typical American experience. An imperious light filled the high sky, a light that granted validity only to the moment, neither the truth of the past nor of the future, a light that blinded us to the question of where we were coming from and where we were going, a light that suffocated all questions of meaning and context beneath its gleaming force. How different from the discreet light that morning! Pleasant to the eyes, gentle and forgiving, but then merciless, too, because it stripped everything of its fake magic, and mercilessly brought out every detail, even the ugly ones, so that things could show themselves as they really were. A light as if made for the calm, fearless, incorruptible recognition of all things, whether strange or our own.

The waiter in yesterday's café had his waistcoat open, it hung carelessly down his body, and he had cigarette ash on his shirt. He was coughing. No, I wouldn't have wanted to swap with him.

I dropped the hire car back in Avignon. Van Vliet held a car key out to me. It wasn't like yesterday, at the paddock in the Camargue. There he had said he wasn't feeling great, which made one think of illness. Now he needed no excuse. He needed no explanation at all. He just gave me the key. I was sure: he knew that I knew why. Our thoughts had dovetailed again. Like yesterday, when the Newfoundland had licked his hand and we both knew that we were thinking of Lea's hands, which had been frightened of everything but animals.

In the car park next to us a young couple were arguing – he spoke German, she French – and insisting on the different languages was like a passage of arms.

'Lea always spoke German to me, with Cécile mostly French,' Van Vliet said as we set off, 'particularly when she was speaking against me to her. In that way my love of Cécile's French turned into a hatred of Lea's French.'

Lea had experienced her progress in a fever. Her triumphs came hot on each other's heels as she overcame technical difficulties. Even her trills got better. Father and daughter were now living in a flat which the tide of notes had turned into a new flat, in which Cécile's absence was discussed increasingly rarely. Lea was less bothered by that than her father was. Then, every now and again, apparently out of the blue, Lea wanted to know all about her mother. Van Vliet sensed that she was comparing her with Marie.

'I realized that nothing of what I said was true. All wrong. *Merde*. After these conversations I lay awake and thought of our first meeting in the cinema. It was shortly after my promotion. *Un homme et une femme*, with Jean-Louis Trintignant, who dashes from the Côte d'Azur to Paris in his car, a whole night long. Cécile's perfume beside me smelled as if it was the perfume of the woman on the screen. The next day I scoured the city until I had it. A perfume by Dior. In the interval we both stayed in our seats and complained about the annoying custom of interrupting a film to sell ice cream. In the street we looked at each other for a moment longer than chance acquaintances usually do. When I think that it was that moment that decided everything, Lea, her happiness and the disaster that it led to. The Royal cinema on Laupenstrasse. A warm summer evening. A bit of moisture on our pupils. My God.

'"Martijn, the romantic cynic!" she said when I talked about Trintignant's bleary face on the way to Paris and the fact that while he drove and drove everything had existed, absolutely everything. "I didn't think that really *existed*!" She said my name in a French accent, no one had ever done that, and I liked it. But a cynic? I don't know why I said that and whether she meant it. I never asked her; there were lots of important things that I never asked her. I noticed that when Lea came with her questions.'

Marie was more important than everything else. Even more than her father. It was only if there were disagreements with Marie and she felt hurt that Lea turned back to him, and when she did so it was to see the steaming, dripping spaghetti on the tennis racquet.

'Lea was growing quickly now, almost by leaps and bounds; she was recognizably the daughter of a tall father. The time came for her first full-size violin. We drove to Zurich, to Lucerne and to a famous violin-maker in St Gallen. Katharina Walther's nose was out of joint, because the selection at Krompholz wasn't enough for me. Marie felt she had been bypassed when we came back with an instrument that looked wonderful and sounded even lovelier. It cost a fortune, and as I stood in the bank, selling shares at a loss, I asked myself with a shiver what I was doing. Even today I can feel how I took my first steps in the street with great care, as if the tarmac might crumble away at any moment. Something within me had started sliding, but I refused to be aware of it and instead decided to organize a little party at home.

'We sat at the kitchen table to draw up the list of invitations. No list came into being. Marie Pasteur at our house? Now, after our upset? Lea pursed her lips and drew patterns on the table top with her finger. I was glad. Caroline? She knew our flat – but as a party guest? Other fellow-pupils, perhaps? The whole class, along with the music teacher? I snapped the notebook shut. We had no friends.

'I made saffron rice, and after we had eaten in silence Lea went to her room to practise on the new violin. It had a warm, golden sound, and after a few minutes it no longer mattered that we had no friends.'

Van Vliet experienced Lea's ambition, her fanaticism and also her coldness when someone got in her way. Markus Gerber had been abandoned long ago. Another boy fell in love with the fourteen-year-old and made the mistake of being given a violin for his birthday. Lea's comments were devastating. On such occasions her father was chilled. But then she came home after an unsuccessful lesson at Marie's, wept, pressed herself against him and was once again the little girl that occasionally said strange, slightly illogical things.

'Then there was the business with Paganini. The fingering he demands is inhuman. Lea showed me what it's supposed to be like. *Il Diablo*, as he was known, had an incredible reach. And he wrote for hands like that. Lea began stretching exercises. Marie forbade them. She went on doing it in secret; she read books about Niccolò. It was only when Marie gave her an ultimatum that she stopped.

'I knew it couldn't go well, I knew all along. The fanaticism. The coldness. The strange statements. I should have talked to Marie. You ask if she, too, didn't notice how dangerous it was getting. But for me . . . *enfin*, it was Marie, I didn't want to . . . And neither did I want Lea's notes to disappear from the flat, the silence would have been terrible. Later I heard it, that terrible silence, that silence of the grave. This evening I will have to hear it again.'

With every passing kilometre we were getting closer to it, that silence in his new and – as he had said – small flat, which, I don't know why, I imagined as being shabby, with a staircase full of unpleasant smells. Involuntarily, I reduced my speed.

'In the time before the first competition that she would take part in, I woke up at dawn and thought: I have forgotten my own life. Since Loyola de Colón I have thought only of Lea's life. Unshaven, I drove through deserted streets to the station. I slowly went down the still-motionless escalator of that time, and tried to imagine what it had been like to be me, before violin music had taken hold of my life. Can one know what things were like before, in the knowledge of what came later? Can one really know that? Or is it more that one gets – is that what happens later – numbed by the convulsive thought that it is what came before?

'I took the public lift up to the university and went to the institute, which was still empty and silent at that early hour. I went through the post and called up my emails. It was all meant for someone that I was, and yet also no longer was. I gave brief answers to two hasty requests, then closed up the office. The titles in front of my name on the office door struck me as particularly ridiculous today, almost vain. Outside the city was waking up. Confused, I realized that I was being drawn towards Monbijou, the district where

I had grown up in a rented block. The forgotten life I was in search of seemed not to be my professional life, but the life before and behind it.

'The block still looked exactly the same. It was up there, on the third floor, that my first professional desire had matured: I wanted to be a counterfeiter. I lay on the bed and imagined all the things one would need to be able to do. It had nothing to do with the fact that my great-grandfather had been a dishonest Dutch banker who fled to Switzerland. I only found that out much later. Banknotes had fascinated me even when I was a little boy. I found it incredible that you could get chocolates in return for a piece of coloured paper. I was surprised beyond measure that no one came running after us and locked us up when we went outside with the chocolates. I found it so incredible that I constantly had to try it out again. I started stealing banknotes from my mother's money box. It was perplexingly easy and risk-free, because she travelled the country with her fashionable swatches and was rarely at home, just as rarely as my father, who did the rounds of doctors with pharmaceutical products. Later I went to see every film about forgery, including the forgery of paintings. I was disappointed and rancorous when the methods of payment I saw every day became increasingly incomprehensible. As soon as I had become acquainted with computers, I took my revenge with plans for an electronic bank robbery. It was incredible that it was now only a matter of using a click to transfer numbers that didn't really exist. I found that even more incredible than the business with the chocolates.

'When my father came back from his trips as a sales rep he was exhausted and irritable. He had no strength and no desire to engage with his boy, a child who had not been planned. But I did find a way to reach him: chess. It meant that you could sit together and didn't have to talk. My father was an impulsive player with brilliant ideas, but without the staying power to employ them against quickly calculating opponents like myself. He lost more and more often. What I will never forget about him is that he was not annoyed about his defeats, but proud of my victories.

'We played in hospital, too. I think he was glad that the mad rush of his life as a salesman was over when his heart was no longer in it. He lived to experience my early doctorate. He grinned. "Dr Martijn van Vliet. Sounds good. Sounds very good. I wouldn't have thought you would do it, when you're always hanging around in chess clubs." My mother, whose swatches had fallen out of fashion, moved to a smaller flat. Before I said goodbye after my weekly visit, I went into her bedroom on some excuse or other and put a few banknotes in her money box. "But you need the money yourself," she said every now and again. "I print it," I said. "Martijn!" She lived to experience Lea's birth. "The idea that you're now a father!" she said. "When you were always such a terrible loner."

'On the Bundesterrasse in Bern two men were playing chess with enormous figures that came up to their knees. They were close to endgame. The old man would lose if he did the obvious thing and took the pawn that was on offer.

He looked at me uncertainly. I shook my head. He moved past the pawn. The young man, who had observed our mute exchange, stared at me. It's better not to do that with me; you can only lose.

'He lost the game after five moves, which I dictated to the old man. The old man would have liked to go for a drink with me, but I was in search of my life and walked on across the Kirchenfeld Bridge to my old secondary school. The pupils, who were a quarter of a century younger than me, were streaming into class. Confused, I realized that I felt excluded when the classroom doors closed. When I used to hold the record for bunking off.

'I stepped into the empty hall, which still smelled of the same floor wax as before. How many simultaneous tournaments had I played in here? I couldn't remember. I had lost only three games in all. "Always against girls," they said with a grin, "and always with short skirts."

'The most fun was to be had playing against Beat Käser, my geography teacher and Hans Lüthi's arch-enemy. Käser was an unimaginative individual with an enormous lower jaw stretched tight with gleaming sin, and emotionally he was one thing above all: a general chief of staff. He would ideally have taught in uniform with a dagger. For him, geography consisted in learning all of the Swiss mountain passes off by heart. He called on me more often than he did the others: "Vliet!" I didn't react, as a matter of principle. Of course, if you're called Käser it leaves a bitter taste to have to call your adversary Van Vliet. When he did so at last, I replied that the Susten led beneath the Aare or the Simplon connected Kandersteg with Kandersteg. He too lost every staring contest, and every time it happened it was enormous fun to watch the way he simply couldn't believe that he had lost again. That man hated me, and he hated me, I think, particularly because of my reputation for being the cheekiest beggar and the slyest bastard in the school, who had sadly to be acknowledged as being brighter than many of the teachers. When I passed Käser's board at the tournament I didn't look at him, just theatrically raised my eyebrows and moved on particularly quickly. He tried to contest the doctor's certificate that excused me from military service. He thought the symptoms were simulated. Which, in fact, they were.

'Later that morning I drove to Lea's school. It was break time when I arrived. Rather than going to her as I had planned and explaining why I had left the house so early, I stood some distance away and watched her. She was standing by the bicycles, absently running her hand along a metal pole. Today it seems to me as if that aimless rubbing was an inconspicuous harbinger of the aimless movement that I saw her making when I discovered her behind the firewood at the Saint-Rémy hospice.

'Now she turned round and walked over to a group of pupils listening to a girl with a raven-black ponytail. The girl looked as if she loved horses, campfires and loud guitar music. A Joan of Arc in the body of a Californian college girl. Klara Kalbermatten from Saas Fee. She could have lifted her mountain bike with one finger, and in other respects she looked as if she was a match for anything. But she had one weak point: her name. Or rather: her hatred of her name. She wanted to be called *Lilli*, Lilli and nothing else, and if someone neglected to comply, she took it as a declaration of war.

'There was a harsh, irreconcilable contrast between the two growing girls, which found expression in different ways: here, Lilli's sun-tanned skin, bursting with health; there, Lea's alabaster complexion, which made her look slightly sickly. Here, Lilli's athletic way of moving, which suggested a swing of the hips at any moment; there, Lea's clumsy way of standing and walking, which might have created the impression that she had forgotten where she had left her limbs. Here, Lilli's direct, steely blue gaze, with unmoving eyelids and the implacability of a straight line; there, Lea's dark, veiled eyes, peeping from the shadow of her long lids. Here, the robust, bronze, ordinary beauty of a surfing mountain queen; there, the pale, aristocratic beauty of a porcelain fairy balancing on the abyss. Lilli would always come out fighting as if it were high noon on a dusty, sun-drenched Main Street; Lea would pretend not even to pick up the gauntlet, before finishing everything off with a sly, lightning-fast manoeuvre from a shadowy ambush. Or was that my own underhand way of doing things? Would she not be more likely to fight Klara Kalbermatten with Cécile's elegance than with my deviousness? With jabs from an invisible foil?

'Over the next few hours I passed by the addresses where I had lived as a student, and stood for a long time outside the rooms of an old chess club that no longer exists. I had paid for part of my studies in there. Martijn the bat, they called me, Martijn the blind worm, because I often played blind against several opponents at once and won half the takings.

'Once, just once, I had a fatal collapse of memory and lost all the games of the evening. After that I didn't play again for six months. More often than usual I called in on my parents in the evening. They were so terribly, so touchingly proud to have a son who studied and who mastered life with such bravura independence. And I wished most devoutly that they would forget all that and be strong, protecting parents to a weak son in a tailspin, for one evening, just one evening. I'd intercepted the warning letters from school, as a latchkey child you have power of the mailbox. How could they have known that everything was not as it seemed?

'By now it was early afternoon. Lea would soon be coming home and I should have been there. But I wanted to go to the cinema. I wanted that repeat of the past as well: to sit down in early afternoon with radiant weather outside for the first showing in the dark cinema and enjoy the feeling of doing something that no one else was doing.'

I saw Tom Courtenay running and triumphantly sitting down before the finishing line, at midday, in the afternoon and at the late show.

'I saw nothing of the film. At first I thought it was because Lea would be coming home to an empty flat as she had done in the morning. But slowly it dawned on me that there was something bigger at stake: I imagined what it would be like if Lea didn't exist at all. If I didn't have to take care of her. Not cook. Not fear a return of her eczema. Not hear her practising. No stage fright. I imagined driving through a night and then standing in front of Marie Pasteur's door. I ran from the cinema and drove home.'

13

NEAR VALENCE we pulled in to a car park so that I could stretch my legs. An icy mistral was blowing down the Rhône Valley. Talking was out of the question. We stood there with our trousers flapping, the biting wind in our faces, which were beginning to sting from the dry cold. 'Could we take a break in Geneva?' Van Vliet had asked before. 'I'd like to go to a bookshop. Payot in Bern went a long time ago.'

I wanted to postpone the moment when he would have to step into his flat and hear the silence, the absence of Lea's notes. 'The silence has followed me there,' he had said of the new flat.

There was, I thought, a practical reason for the move: he now lived alone. Perhaps he had also been trying to escape the past. And yet there had been something in his voice, a kind of resentment, as if someone had forced him to switch to the smaller flat. As if some authority had exercised power over him. It must have been a powerful authority, I thought. Van Vliet wasn't the kind of man who would allow himself simply to be driven from his flat.

'There was this music teacher,' he said as we drove on. 'Josef Valentin. An unremarkable, almost invisible man. Small, mouse-grey suits, waistcoat, colourless ties. Thin hair. Only his eyes were anything special: dark brown, always somehow looking surprised, concentrated. And he wore an excessively large signet ring that everyone laughed at because it didn't suit him at all. The pupils called him Joe – an impossible name for him, and that was why they called him it. When he stood on the podium and conducted the school orchestra, he always risked looking ridiculous; he was simply too small and too thin; every movement looked as if he were protesting against his inconspicuousness. But when he went to the piano, the giggles made way for respectful silence. Then his hands were so nimble and strong that even the ring seemed justified.

'He loved Lea. Loved her with all his timid being, which only emerged through music. Old man loves beautiful girl – somehow it was quite natural, but then again not. He never stood too close to her, quite the contrary, he shrank away when she appeared, it was a distance of admiration and untouchability; and I think he might have forgotten himself if he had had to watch anyone pressurizing Lea. "He calls Lilli Fräulein Kalbermatten," Lea told me. "I have a feeling he does it for me." After her school leaving exam she sometimes talked about him. Then you could tell that she missed his contact-free affection and admiration.

'He and Marie didn't like each other. No hostility. But they avoided greeting one another at school concerts. If they were both in the room you could tell they were thinking: it would be better if the other didn't exist.

'Lea outdid herself from one school concert to the next. She never made another mistake as she had with the Rondo. She still had red patches on her throat before performing, and between movements she inevitably wiped her hand on her dress. But her confidence grew. None the less I suffered and trembled at each difficult passage. I knew them all from home.

'At the age of sixteen she played Bach's E major Violin Concerto with the school orchestra. She told me about the rehearsals through gritted teeth. The girl who played first violin in the orchestra was two years older than Lea. She talked about herself as the "concert master" and could hardly bear the fact that Lea was the soloist. Her instrument didn't sound as good as Lea's. When she stood opposite me after the concert, she looked at me with an expression that said: it's just because they had the cash to buy her that instrument.

'There were two small fluffs in Lea's performance that made Marie flinch. Otherwise it was a brilliant performance with thundering applause and stamping. Marie had tears in her eyes and touched my arm as she had never done before. Someone took a photograph of Lea in the long, red dress that she had chosen with Marie.' Van Vliet gulped. 'It's one of the pictures I don't know whether to throw away, tear up or just lock away.'

Before we turned off towards Geneva, near Lyon, Van Vliet said into the silence: 'Joe put Lea forward for the competition in St Moritz. If only he hadn't done that. *If only he hadn't done that!*'

14

LEA WAS LET OFF school for the last two weeks before the competition, he told me. She spent most of her time with Marie, who had cancelled all her other lessons. They were rehearsing a Bach sonata. Again and again they listened to the way Itzhak Perlman played it. Sometimes they worked until late into the night, and then Lea stayed at Marie's. 'His Stradivariuses – no one else has a chance,' she is supposed to have said of Perlman's violin. Those words must have echoed through Van Vliet.

He dreamed the eczema had come back, and sometimes he woke, drenched in sweat, because he saw Lea on stage in front of him, vainly trying to remember the next few bars.

'We met two days before the start of the competition in St Moritz. It was late January and the snow was incessant. Lea's room lay between Marie's and mine. In the hotel ballroom they had just finished setting up the technical side of things. We gave a start when we saw the television cameras. Lea went on stage and stayed there for a long time. Every now and again she wiped her hands on her dress. She would like to practise now, she said after that, and then she and Marie went upstairs.

'I can still feel the snow from that time on my face. It helped me to survive those days. I hired cross-country skis and was out for hours. Cécile and I had often done that. Silently, side by side, we had followed our trail through the thick snow, far from the usual routes. It was on one of those trips that we first talked about children.

'Children were out of the question for me, I said. Cécile stopped. "But why?"

'I had prepared for this question for a long time. Hands resting on my poles, head lowered, I uttered the words that I had prepared.

'"I don't want the responsibility. I don't know how it works: taking responsibility for other people. I don't even know how to do it for myself."

'I didn't progress beyond such phrases. Even today I don't know what Cécile did with them. Whether she understood them; whether she took them seriously. When she told me, a good year after our wedding, that Lea was on the way, I was scared stiff. But she had become my anchor and I didn't want to lose her.

'It was nine years since I had last closed the door to her sickroom, quietly, as if she could still hear. "You must promise me that you'll look after . . . " she had said the day before. "Yes," I had cut in, "yes, of course." After that I was sorry that I hadn't let her finish. Even now, as the rising wind drove the snowflakes into my face, I choked on it. I slid back to the hotel at a rate of knots.

'At her first performance, stage fright had been something that had afflicted Lea like an illness that you can't do anything about. In the six years that had passed in the meantime, she had learned to outwit it by undertaking lots of other things that kept her busy when a performance approached. And if she was playing at school, to my surprise it helped if Klara Kalbermatten and her disciples were sitting in the audience. Lilli was furious about the glamour that Lea could lend to a party. Admittedly, she won all the races on the running track and in the pool; but she sensed that that wasn't enough as a counterweight. Lea knew that, and when Lilli flopped down in the front row in scruffy clothing, she lost all dread, enjoyed the situation and mastered all technical difficulties as if they simply didn't exist.

'In St Moritz it was all different. If she won this competition, she could think of a career as a soloist. I was against such a career. I didn't want to have to watch Lea being devoured by stage fright, by annoyance over press reports and by fear of having damp hands. Above all, however, I didn't want to tremble every time I remembered her. And there were reasons to tremble. Nothing serious had happened since the mistake in the Rondo, nothing that could have been compared with my collapse in chess. The notes had never been engulfed by sudden forgetfulness, the fingers had never stiffened because they didn't know where to slide to next. But once, when she was playing a Mozart sonata, she started playing the third movement before the second, and once it seemed as if she thought she'd finished after the second. Joe at the grand piano had excellent self-control and stripped the mistake of its embarrassment with a warm, paternal smile. "Sorry," Lea had said. I had dreamed of it and I never wanted to hear that "sorry" again. Never again.

'In the hotel dining room all ten competitors sat under chandeliers and pretended to take no notice of one another. There were big gaps between the ten tables, and the ones who would be trying to trump one another with their violins the following day spoke to the people in charge with exaggerated liveliness and enthusiasm, it seemed to me, as if to demonstrate that they weren't even slightly concerned about the presence of their rivals.

'Lea said nothing and darted occasional glances at the other tables. She was wearing the high-necked black dress that she had bought with Marie while I was out in the snow. It was the dress that she would also wear at her performance. The high collar would hide the red patches of agitation on her throat. Suddenly, Lea couldn't bear those patches and they had hung up the shoulderless dress she had planned to wear and gone in search of another. The new dress gave her head, with its pinned-up hair, a certain nun-like severity that reminded me of Marie Curie.

'We were the first to leave the dining room. When Lea had closed the door of her room behind her, I was standing in the corridor with Marie. It was the first time I'd seen her smoking.

'"You don't want Lea to win," she said.

'I gave a start, as if I'd been caught stealing.

'"Am I so easy to read?"

'"Only where Lea is concerned," she said with a smile.

'I would have liked to ask her what she hoped for, and what she thought of Lea's chances. There were lots of things I should have asked her. She must have seen it on my face, because she raised her eyebrows.

'"Till tomorrow, then," I said and left.

'From the window of my room I looked out over snow-covered St Moritz at night. Light still came from Lea's room. I repeated the words I had said to Cécile about responsibility. I had no idea what was right. Dawn was already breaking by the time I finally fell asleep.'

15

As we got closer to Geneva, dusk began to fall beneath dark clouds. Van Vliet had gone to sleep with his head turned towards me. He smelled of alcohol and tobacco. While telling me about Lea's performance in St Moritz, he had taken out his hip flask and lit one cigarette from the glowing tip of the last. No one's allowed to smoke in my own car, I can't bear it. And it's particularly bad when I haven't had much sleep. Already I could hardly breathe and I could smell the smoke in my clothes. But it didn't matter now. Somehow it didn't matter.

I looked at him. He hadn't shaved this morning, and he was wearing the same shirt whose collar he had tugged on the previous day when he was swearing at the tourists who wanted to see Van Gogh's room in the hospice. An un-ironed shirt of unidentifiable colour, washed a thousand times, the three top buttons open at the top. A battered black jacket. He was breathing through his mouth and nose at the same time and a quiet rattle accompanied the breaths that he seemed to be struggling to make.

With his eyes closed he looked as if he were in need of protection. Not like someone who had wanted to be a forger and who had destroyed a chess opponent on the Bundesterrasse because he dared to stare at him. More like someone who had feared Ruth Adamek, even though he would never have admitted it. And above all like someone who hadn't wanted to assume responsibility for a child, because he had the feeling that he didn't want to assume responsibility for himself. And like someone who had felt so lashed by the words of Dr Meridjen that he could speak of him only as *the Maghrebi*.

I tried to imagine Tom Courtenay asleep and wondered what it would be like if he lived with a daughter consumed by a threatening passion for violin-playing. Van Vliet had lost all certainties about that. 'I no longer even seemed to know my way around the lab,' he had said.

The candidates in the competition had played in alphabetical order. That meant that Lea was second to last.

'She was pale and her smile was uneasy as she sat down with us at the breakfast table. No one was forced to listen to the other competitors, but when I suggested taking a walk instead, Lea grumpily dismissed the idea. She wouldn't listen to a word I said that day and once I caught myself thinking about leaving the hotel without an explanation, driving to

Kloten and boarding the nearest plane. In fact, I sat beside her every minute when the lights dimmed over the audience. We didn't exchange a single word and didn't look at each other, and yet at every second I knew what Lea was thinking. I heard it in her breathing and sensed it in the way she sat there, shifting on her chair. They were hours of torment and at the same time hours in which I was happy about the proximity created by that wordless deciphering of her innermost being.

'The playing of the first two candidates was stiff and uncommunicative. I sensed Lea relaxing. I was happy to sense it. But in retrospect I was startled by the cruelty hidden behind her relaxation. From now on I was filled with contradictory feelings of that kind. Other people's weaknesses meant hope, and the relief that was audible in Lea's deep breaths meant cruelty.

'What was it like when I played a game of chess that really mattered? I saw my father in front of me, moving the pieces with his liver-spotted hand. "How do you do that?" he sighed with feigned resignation when he saw that defeat could no longer be averted. Once, when I saw my own defeat coming and resigned, leaving the king on his side, he reached quickly and violently for the piece and put it back up again. He wasn't the man who could explain something like that. But his face suddenly looked white and angular, as if carved in marble, and I understood that behind his fatigue and weariness there was an unbending pride. In his silent, exhausted way he had taught me what it's like to want to win, without that will including a readiness to be cruel. More than twenty years had passed since he had last given me his hand in the ward and pressed it more firmly than usual, as if he had sensed that he was going to die in the night.

'I had wordlessly – wordlessly even deep within – resented him for never being there; now I had never missed him as much as I did in that moment, when I sat beside my daughter, hoping tensely for the others to fail. How do you pass on experiences to a child? What do you do when you discover a cruelty in that child, a cruelty that frightens you?

'Two of the five candidates who had played in the morning hadn't appeared for lunch. The three others bent shyly and silently over their plates. They must have noticed that their playing had been far from brilliant, and now they had to endure the looks of the others who had heard it as well. I looked from one to the other. Children who had played like adults and were now eating their soup like children. My God, I thought, how cruel.

'The parents also knew that it hadn't been enough. A mother stroked her daughter's hair, a father rested his hand on his son's shoulder. And then, very suddenly, it became clear to me that it is *always* cruel when other people's eyes rest on us; even if those looks are benevolent. They turn us into actors. We can no longer be ourselves, we have to be there for others who want to lead us away from ourselves. And the worst is: we must pretend to be someone quite particular. The others expect it. But at the same time we *are* perhaps not that person. Perhaps what we want is *not* to be someone particular and hide ourselves in a reassuring vagueness.'

I thought of Paul's uncomprehending look above the face mask, which had made me shrink back into myself. And the face of the nurse who had cast her eyes down. The fact that she hadn't been able to bear seeing me in a moment of weakness had been even worse than Paul's horror.

'The afternoon began with a surprise. A girl with the fairy-tale name of Solvejg stepped on stage. Her freckled face seemed never to have known a smile. Her dress hung down her body like a sack and her arms were pitifully thin. I involuntarily expected a feeble stroke and a thin tone that would make us all cringe.

'And then that explosion! A Russian composer, I didn't know the name. A firework display with breath-taking switches of level, glissandi and double-stopping. The girl's hair, which had looked unwashed and stringy, suddenly flew, her eyes flashed and her frail body supply followed the musical tension. There was complete silence in the room. The applause exceeded everything we had heard in the morning. It was clear to everyone: the competition had just begun.

'Lea had sat there motionless. I hadn't heard her breathing. I looked at Marie. Yes, her expression seemed to say, this was what she would be measured against. Lea had closed her eyes. She slowly rubbed her thumbs against one another. I felt an impulse to stroke her hair and put my arm around her shoulder. When had I begun to suppress such impulses? When, in fact, had I last hugged her, my daughter?

'Another two candidates until it was her turn. The girl tripped over the hem of her dress, the boy kept wiping his hands on his trousers; on his pale face you could see the fear that his damp fingers might slip on the strings. When the boy started playing I went outside.

'When I got up I had looked at neither Lea nor Marie. There was nothing to explain. It was flight. A flight from the trepidation of these children, who had been told by someone important to travel here and expose themselves to the eyes and ears of the competitors and the judges. The oldest was twenty, the youngest sixteen. JEUNESSE MUSICALE – the town was full of those letters, which looked lovely and peaceful, golden varnish washing over a lowering anxiety, suffocating ambition and damp hands. Off the road, I stamped through the thick snow. When I saw a line of waiting taxis I thought again of Kloten Airport. Lea would see my empty seat from the stage. I cooled my face with snow. When I stepped into the room half an hour later with wet trousers, Lea was already in the waiting room. Marie said nothing when I sat down.'

16

'IT WAS SIX YEARS since I first sat in the school hall and first saw Lea on stage. Is it like that for everyone, that a great anxiety never dissolves, it just disappears behind the backdrop before emerging again later on, its power unbroken? Is it like that for you? And why is it different where joy, hope and happiness are concerned? Why are the shadows so much more powerful than the light? Can you explain that to me, damn it all?'

His expression, I think, was supposed to be full of irony – the expression of someone who could still distance himself from his grief and despair. An expression like the one I saw outside the open lift yesterday. An expression like Tom Courtenay's when he was the only one no one visited on visiting days. But Van Vliet wasn't strong enough, and it turned into an expression filled with pain and incomprehension, the expression of a boy looking for a place to linger in his father's eyes. As if I were the kind of person who would give such an expression a good reception.

'You're so strong in your white coat,' Leslie had once said, 'and yet it's still impossible to cling to you.'

I was glad when a motorway toll gate came and I had to look for money. When we drove on, Van Vliet's voice sounded firmer again.

'When the lights went out and Lea stepped on stage, Marie crossed herself with her thumb in the dark. Perhaps it was only my imagination, but the silence seemed to be even more complete than it had been before the others played. It was the silence of a cloister, I thought, an invisibly besieged cloister. Perhaps I thought it partly because in her high-necked black dress and with her hair pinned up Lea looked like a novice, a girl who had left everything behind her and dedicated herself entirely to the holy Mass of notes.

'More slowly than I had seen her do it before, she put the white cloth over the violin's chin-rest, checked it, corrected it and checked it again. The seconds stretched out. I thought of the Rondo and of Lea saying that she wanted to hurl the violin into the audience. Now she checked the tension of the bow again, then she closed her eyes, adjusted her fingering and put the bow to the strings. The spotlights seemed to become very slightly brighter. What happened now would determine Lea's future. I forgot to breathe.

'That my daughter could play such music! Music of such purity, warmth and depth! I tried to find a word and after a while it came to me: *sacred*. She played the Bach sonata as if she were building a sacred object with each individual note. The notes were appropriately immaculate: certain, pure and unshakeable, they cut the silence, which, the longer the playing lasted, seemed to become even bigger and deeper. I thought of the sounds of Loyola de Colón in the station, of Lea's first, scratchy notes in our flat, of the confidence that Marie's notes had had at their first meeting. Marie wiped the sweat from her forehead with a handkerchief. I smelled her perfume and felt the warmth of her body. She was the one who had turned my little daughter into a woman, who knew how to fill the hotel ballroom with that overwhelming beauty. For a moment I took her hand and she returned my pressure.'

Van Vliet was drinking. A few drops ran down his chin. It may sound strange, but those drops, that sign of lost control, allowed me to guess how terrible it must have been, the fall that led from that glorious moment in the ballroom in St Moritz to Lea's stay in the hospice of Saint-Rémy, where Van Vliet had seen his daughter behind the stack of firewood, absently running her thumb along the tip of her index finger. *Elle est brisée dans son âme*, the doctor had said. The Maghrebi.

'As I said: sacred,' Van Vliet went on now, and then fell silent again for a while. 'Later, when I knew more, I sometimes thought: She had played as if she were building an imaginary cathedral of notes, in which she could sometimes seek refuge when life became too much for her. I thought that above all on the trip to Cremona. And then I sat in the Duomo there, as if it were that imaginary cathedral.' He swallowed. 'It was lovely, thinking that crazed thought again and again, morning, afternoon and evening. It was as if I were able to establish a connection with the aberrant way in which Lea was now thinking and feeling. Sometimes, in fact, in a hidden, sealed chamber deep within me, I envied Lea the stubbornness that led her away from everything ordinary and reasonable. In my dream I was with her behind the firewood in Saint-Rémy. The contours of all things, including our own, blurred and dissolved as if in a watercolour of pallid, over-diluted colours. It was a precious dream that I managed to cling to into the next day.'

And this was the man, I reflected, who had been saved by books about Marie Curie and Louis Pasteur, the man whose scientific, algorithmic intelligence had made him the youngest professor at Bern University.

'Lea bowed. I thought back to her first bow, way back then, after the Rondo. I told you what had worried me about it: she had bowed as if the world had no other *choice* but to cheer her; as if she could *demand* applause. The young woman who had taken the place of the little girl demanded the same thing. But now it seemed much more dangerous than before: it would somehow have been possible to explain to the little girl that listeners had their own judgement; no one could have explained that to the seventeen-year-old Lea standing there on the ballroom stage. No one at all.

'Was the applause louder and longer than it had been for Solvejg? I knew that Lea, while she made her curt, almost imperious bows, which still had something clumsy about them, would be able to think only of that one question. That she lived through each individual second in the apprehensive hope that the applause might reach undiminished into the next second and continue even after that, second after second, until it became quite clear that it had outdone the long, enthusiastic clapping after Solvejg's performance.

'That was what I would have liked to keep from my daughter: that breathless listening into the audience, that feverish need for applause and appreciation, that addiction to admiration and the poison of disappointment if the applause was weaker and briefer than it had been in the imagination.

'Her face was covered with a film of sweat when she came to us afterwards. She didn't want to hear Alexander Zacharias, the last candidate, she said with a resolution behind which one sensed fear and vulnerability. So we left the hotel and stepped outside into a thick snowstorm. Neither Marie nor I dared to ask how her performance had gone. One word out of place and she would shatter. While our shoes crunched on the snow, I thought back once again to the moment in Bern railway station, when little Lea had suddenly resisted my attempt to draw her to me.

'"I would like to be like Dinu Lipatti," she said after a while. Later Marie told me about this Romanian pianist and we wondered what Lea might have meant. Had she mixed him up with George Enescu, the Romanian violinist? I bought a CD of Dinu Lipatti. When I heard her in the empty flat, I tried to imagine how Lipatti would have sounded as a violinist. Yes, I thought, yes, exactly. But I was pursuing a phantom, one of the many phantoms who determined my actions, a whole army of phantoms. Lea really had mixed up Lipatti with Enescu. She refused to admit it and stamped her feet. I showed her the CD. She threw open the window and hurled it outside. Simply threw it out of the window. The crash that came as the plastic cover hit the tarmac was terrible.'

Van Vliet fell silent for a moment. There was a distant echo of his former horror in that silence. 'That was after David Lévy had entered her life and destroyed everything.'

17

WITH DAVID LÉVY a new calendar began in the life of father and daughter. And with the mention of his name a new chapter began in Van Vliet's narrative, or rather in his narration. Because what was new was above all the violence and disorder with which he now spoke of all the things that had been raging in him for years. Hitherto there had been a sequence of narration that revealed an ordering hand, a director of memory. From this moment on, it seemed to me, there was only a rushing stream of images, scraps of thoughts and feelings, which broke its banks and tore away with it everything else that he still was. He had even forgotten to tell me the outcome of the competition, and I had to remind him.

'There was complete silence in the hall as the chair of the jury came on stage to announce the result of their deliberations. His movements were hesitant and it was clear that he felt sorry for the candidates that he would have to disappoint. He put on his glasses and awkwardly unfolded the sheet of paper bearing the names of the first three candidates. He would start with third place. Lea's fingers were convulsively intertwined and she seemed to be barely breathing.

'Solvejg Lindström was third. Again, she surprised me and threw my expectations back at me like shabby prejudices. I had expected disappointment and a thin, courageous smile. But her freckled face beamed; she enjoyed the applause and bowed gracefully, even her dress looking neat and tidy now. She was the least conspicuous of them all and the least presumptuous. But she was also, I thought, the most self-controlled, and when I compared her with my daughter, tensed to the utmost, it gave me a pang.

'Where the first and second places were concerned, the chairman said, the jury had argued for a long time. Both candidates had impressed with both technical brilliance and depth of interpretation. In the end the decision had been: Alexander Zacharias in first place, Lea van Vliet in second place.

'And then it happened: while Zacharias leapt to his feet and hurried on stage, Lea sat where she was. I turned to her. I will never forget her empty gaze. Was it just the emptiness of a paralysing disappointment? Or did it contain indignation and fury, which kept her frozen to her chair? Marie rested her hand on her shoulder and gestured to her to get up. Then she rose to her feet at last and went clumsily up to the stage.

'The applause for Zacharias had already ebbed away, the new applause for Lea was dull, with a hint of disapproval. Perhaps only surprised, perhaps also reluctant, Lea took the hands of the other two contestants and bowed with them. It hurt, it hurt so terribly to see my daughter up there between the other two, forcing her into a bow, which – it was clear to everybody – she didn't want and which was much more curt and stiff than the bows of the others. She looked so alone up there, alone and exposed, exposed by herself, and I thought about how we had sat in the kitchen on the evening after the purchase of the violin and realized that we had no friends to celebrate with.'

After that Van Vliet had fallen silent and finally gone to sleep. In Geneva I drove straight to a hotel that I knew. He had never cared about a bookshop. He had only ever cared about having to go back to his silent flat, where Lea's notes could no longer be heard.

I woke him and pointed to the hotel. 'I'm too tired to go on driving,' I said. He looked at me and nodded. He knew I had seen through him.

'That was my last journey to Saint-Rémy,' he said over dinner. He gazed out at the lake. 'Yes, I think that was the last journey.'

It might have meant that he now felt free of the compulsion to return repeatedly to the place where he had seen Lea crouching behind the firewood. It might have meant that the struggle with the Maghrebi was over at last. But it might also have meant something else. I watched the burning tip eat through the paper of his cigarette. From the side it was impossible to tell from his face what meaning the words had. Whether they were the relaxed words of a conclusion or whether they heralded something new.

He stubbed out his cigarette. 'I didn't see him coming to our table – Lévy, I mean. Suddenly he was just standing there, without a word of greeting, self-confident, a man to whom the world belonged, and addressed his words to Lea. "*Une décision injuste*," he said, "*j'ai lutté pour vous.*" He has a melodious voice that also carries when he's speaking quietly. Lea swallowed her food and looked up at him: a light grey suit made of fine fabric, perfectly cut, waistcoat with watch chain, full, salt-and-pepper hair, goatee beard, gold-rimmed glasses, a hint of eternal youth in his face. "*Your playing: sublime, superb, a miracle.*" I saw the gleam in Lea's eyes, and then I knew: she would go away with him into the French language, Cécile's language, which for so long she had been unable to speak.

'Lévy seduced my daughter away into that language. From now on Lea, too, used the word *sublime*, a word that I had never heard Cécile utter. And it wasn't just that word, there were others, too, rare, choice words which assembled themselves into a new space in which my daughter began to live.

'His staccato of verbless admiration – it had struck me as stilted, mannered, vain. That linguistic gesture on its own would have been enough to turn me against him. Much later, during an encounter after which everything suddenly looked very different, I understood that that style was part of him, like the waistcoat, the watch chain, the English shoes. That he was a man from a French chateau, who knew by heart Proust and Apollinaire. That wherever he went he would always be surrounded by a chateau, by Gobelin tapestries, furniture made of the choicest woods, gleaming and impeccable. And that when he knew unhappiness, it would be the unhappiness of the disappointed, lonely owner of a chateau, above whose head the beams in the high ceilings were becoming rotten and unsound, the chandeliers, dull and stained, turning to brass and glass.

'" *Vous voulez faire un petit tour ensemble*?" He could see that Lea was in the middle of dinner, that we all were. He could *see*. "*Avec plaisir*," Lea said and got to her feet.

'I knew straight away that that was how it would always be from now on: that she would get to her feet in the middle of dinner and in the middle of everything else. He took her hand and made to kiss it. I froze. His lips were at least ten centimetres way from touching her hand. Ten centimetres, at least. And it was only a ritual, a pale memory of a kiss. Pure convention. Still.

'He turned to us, a brief glance, the hint of a bow. "*Marie. Monsieur.*"

'Marie and I set aside our knives and forks and pushed away our plates. It was as if our time had been cut off, right in front of our noses. Lea had turned around to us before she left, a hint of guilt in her eyes. Then she had gone out with Lévy, out from the life that she had led with me and Marie, into a life with a man she had known nothing about five minutes ago, a man who would lead her to dizzying heights and later to the edge of the abyss. My stomach felt like a lump of lead and my head was filled with dull, thoughtless silence.

'Through the glass door of the dining room we saw Lévy waiting for Lea in the foyer. When she walked up to him she was wearing her coat. Her hair, which had always been pinned up until now, was loose. Her pinned-up hair had been like a restrained, tamed energy, and like a renunciation: all her strength, all her love was to flow into the notes. Now, along with her wavy hair, her body, too, was flowing into the world, not just her talent. I thought her playing might now lose its power. But the opposite happened: her tone itself acquired a physical quality, a sensual weight that was new. I often yearned for her cool, sacred brittleness. It had been such a good, such a perfect match for Lea's nun-like beauty, which was washed away by the surge of her flowing hair.

'She walked through the foyer with Lévy and out into the night.

'Nothing would be as it had been before. I felt slightly dizzy. It was as if the dining room, the hotel and the whole town were losing their ordinary, compact reality and turning into the backdrop of a bad dream.

'Only now did I notice how much Marie's face had changed. It was red, almost feverish, and there was something harsh and implacable about her features. *Marie.* They knew each other. The look he had given her had been a look without warmth, unsmiling, a look that greeted her over a big distance in time. It had expressed a memory of something dark and bitter, but also a willingness to let things lie.

'"Is he a violinist too?" I asked. She threw her hands over her face. Her breath was halting. Now she looked at me. It was a strange look and only retrospectively did I manage to decipher it: it contained pain and bitterness, but also a spark of admiration and – I don't know – even more than that.

'"*The* violinist," she said. "*The* violinist of Switzerland. Above all of French Switzerland. There was no one better, back then, twenty years ago. That was what most people thought, and he showed no doubt that he thought it too. Rich father, who bought him an Amati violin. But it wasn't just the instrument. It was his hands. The organizers would have been able to sell out any concert he played five, ten times over. DAVID LÉVY – back then the name had an unsurpassed glamour."

'She lit a cigarette and then rubbed her lighter with her thumb for a long time, without saying anything.

'"Then came Geneva, a memory lapse in the Oistrakh cadenza of the Beethoven Concerto, he flees the hall, the papers are full of it. After that he never appeared in public again. Nothing more was heard of him for years. Rumours about psychiatric treatment. Then, about ten years ago, he started teaching. He developed into a phenomenal teacher, all of his charisma now flowed into teaching, and he was given a masterclass in Bern. He stopped all of a sudden, no one could work out why. He retreated into his house in Neuchâtel. Every now and again I heard of someone taking lessons from him, but they must have been exceptions. Over the last two or three years I've never heard anything more about him. I had no idea that he was sitting on the jury here."

'She was sure that he would offer Lea lessons. "The way he looked at her," she said. And she was sure that Lea would do it. "I know her. Then it will be the second time that I've lost to him."

'For the next little while I was constantly about to ask her what the first defeat had been. And whether that was why she didn't perform as a soloist or in an orchestra. But at the last moment something warned me against it. Then eventually it was too late, so I never found out.

'When we were standing outside her room she looked at me. "It won't happen the way you may be thinking," she said. "With him and Lea, I mean. I'm sure of it. He isn't that kind of man."

'*He isn't that kind of man*. How often would I say those words over the next few years!

'The following day Lévy took her to Neuchâtel in his green Jaguar.

'"It means we can get to work straight away," Lea said. She was sitting in my room, after coming back from her walk with him, her hair damp with snow. I hadn't known that staying calm could be such an effort. She saw that. "It's . . . it's OK, isn't it?"

'I looked at her and felt as if I were seeing her family face for the first time. The face that had developed out of the face of my little daughter, who had listened breathlessly to

Loyola de Colón in the railway station. The face of a little girl, a teenager, and a young, ambitious woman who had just met a man whom she hoped would give her a brilliant future. All in one. Should I have forbidden it? Could I have forbidden it? What would it have done to the two of us? And I'm not even sure if she wouldn't have done it anyway, there was that flush to her face, that energy, that hope. I can't remember what I said. When she kissed me on the cheek I stood there as if I was made of wood. She hesitated at the door for a moment and turned her head. Then she was outside.

'I spent most of that night sitting by the window, looking out into the snow. At first I wondered how she would tell Marie. And then, all of a sudden, I guessed: she wouldn't tell her at all. Not out of cold-bloodedness. Out of insecurity and anxiety and guilt. And because she simply didn't know how to express such a thing, certainly not to the woman who had replaced her mother and who had been her guiding star for eight years. The longer I thought about it, the greater my certainty became: she would set off without having talked to Marie.

'I had a feeling in my gut. I saw Lea writing postcards to Marie in Rome and trying to phone her to tell her the cards were on the way. Doing what she was about to do was the coward's way out. I ran through a series of excuses in my head, but the feeling remained. It took years for it to fade. "A Dutchman doesn't run away from anything," my father used to say when he saw cowardice. It was kitsch and nonsense, particularly since he himself was a total wimp often enough, and on top of everything we hadn't been Dutchmen for an eternity. During that night I thought of his silly saying and I liked it, even though, in fact, it only made everything worse.

'It happened as I had expected. I saw it when I joined Marie at the breakfast table, where only two places had been set. "She's only seventeen," I said. She nodded. But it hurt her, my God how it hurt her.

'When Lea received a package containing the golden ring from the merry-go-round a few days later – only the ring, not a single word – I saw Marie's face at the breakfast table in front of me, a weary, disappointed, lifeless face.

'Lea stared at the ring without touching it. She stared and stared, her face filled with horror and disbelief. Then she got to her feet, the chair fell over, she ran to her room and wept like a little child.

'I felt: I should go to her and comfort her. But it was out of the question. Completely out of the question. And I was so disturbed by it that I left my weeping child alone in the flat and walked through the city to Monbijou, where I had lain in bed as a boy and dreamed of being a forger. *I don't want this responsibility. I don't know how it works: assuming responsibility for someone.* Why didn't you respect that? I said to Cécile. I wasn't just talking off the top of my head. You must have sensed that too, so why?

'I saw just how wounded Marie really was as we walked to my car in the car park in St Moritz. As we passed a green

Jaguar, Marie took out her bunch of keys, chose the most pointed one and with a swift motion scratched a scar in the paint of the car. After taking a few steps she went back, and this time she drew the key the full length of the car, from the back to the front bumper. I couldn't believe my eyes, and looked around to see if anyone had seen. An elderly couple were looking over at us. Marie put the keys away. Go on, arrest me, her face said, I don't care now anyway.

'"She got into one of those with him this morning," she said as I drove off. "Not a word. Not a single word."

'We drove in silence, and every now and again she wiped quiet tears from her eyes.

'We clung to one another. Yes, I think that's the right word: we clung to one another. We did so with a kind of stubborn violence that might be seen as uninhibited passion; in fact, at first, that was what we thought it was. Until the despair in it could no longer be denied. On the evening of the drive home from St Moritz I sat at Marie's on the sofa with all the cushions and the gleaming chintz. She was wearing a pale, faded pink batik dress scattered with fine Asian characters, as if painted with a brush and, as on the evening of our first visit, soft leather slippers which were like a second skin. She had come in, set down the suitcase and, still in her coat, walked to the grand piano on which Lea's sheet music lay. She sorted Lea's scores out from the rest, shuffled them with meticulous care into a clean pile and carried them from the room. She had hesitated for a moment and I had thought she was going to hand them to me so that I could take them home, since they would never again be played in this flat. But then she had carried them outside and I had heard the sound of a drawer.'

Van Vliet paused and turned his face towards the lake, his eyes closed. He must have seen the image he now had before his eyes thousands of times before. It was an image that carried enormous weight, and it still caused him so much pain that he hesitated to speak of it.

'Lea always laid a cloth, a white cloth, over the chin-rest of the violin. She had many such cloths; we found the shop where they could be bought together. One of those cloths lay on the window sill. When Marie came back in she looked around the room and found it. She carried it outside. I'm sure she didn't want me to see it, but her desire was too strong, so it happened in the doorway, still within my field of vision: she smelled the cloth. She pressed her nose firmly into it, raised her other hand as well and pressed the whole cloth into her face. She tottered a bit, standing there, blindly devoted to Lea's smell.'

He never showed me a picture of Marie. And yet I can see her in front of me, her face pressed into the cloth. I just need to close my eyes and already I can see her. She has bright eyes filled with devotion, wherever she looks.

'We puzzled over whether the characters on her dress were Japanese or Korean. Marie turned out the light. We sensed the emptiness that Lea left in the room that she had filled with her notes. And then we clung to one another, suddenly, violently, and only let go again when it was light outside.'

He smiled the way Tom Courtenay could smile, in the midst of his unhappiness. 'Love for the sake of a third party. Love arising out of entangled abandonment. As a bulwark against the pain of parting. Love, which is not actually meant for the other. A love which, as far as I'm concerned, was lived at a nine-year delay, in the shadow of the knowledge of that delay, a shadow which meant that feelings gradually faded away. And what about her? Was I just the bond that linked her to a lost Lea? A guarantee that Lea wasn't quite out of the world? For both of us it was a long time since we had hugged somebody. Did she want, with my longing, to suffocate her own longing for Lea? I don't know. Do we know *anything*?

'Six months ago I saw her in the distance. She's fifty-three now, not an old woman, but she looked tired and wiped out. "Thank you for bringing me Lea," she said the last time we saw each other. The words caught in my throat. I dreamed of them. Even today I sometimes wake up and think I heard them in my sleep.

'Did she understand what had happened? To Lea and then to me? It was Marie, after all. The woman who always looked for clarity. The woman with the passion of understanding. The woman who always wanted to know why people did what they did, and wanted to know very precisely. But perhaps this time she didn't *want* to know. Perhaps she needed not to understand, as a bulwark against pain and abandonment. Apart from those words of farewell we never spoke of Lea again, not once. At first she was present between us through her numbing absence. Then, gradually, that absence faded too. In Marie's rooms Lea became a spectre.'

Van Vliet came back from the toilet. We ordered the third bottle of wine. He had drunk most of it.

'I don't want to blame Lévy. He was just a misfortune for Lea, a great misfortune. The way it can be a misfortune for one person to meet another.

'But I can only see that today. Back then it was quite different. It made me ill that she was driving to Neuchâtel every other day. *He isn't that kind of man.* I think Marie was right. I was on the lookout. Searching for signs. She was buying clothes and didn't want me to be there. Lipstick that she wiped away before she came into the house. I saw that. She grew a little more, her body filled out. Every time she came back from seeing him she seemed to bring back more of the courtly aura, the castellan glamour which had, in the meantime, settled over the whole town of Neuchâtel in my mind. It was as if she were acquiring a kind of patina, a sheen produced by playing the violin with Lévy. I hated it, that pretentious, stinking, money-stinking patina. I hated the evident progress that Lea was making. I hated it when she said, "Right, then, I'm off," in a tone in which I could already hear the French that she would shortly be speaking with him. I hated her railway season ticket, her small, crumpled timetable and – yes, I hated Lévy, David Lévy, whom she called David. Once, when I could no longer control myself and rummaged around in her things, I found a notebook with a page on which she had written over and over again, LEA LÉVY.

'Still, the thing that I had feared didn't happen. I would have noticed it. I don't know why, but I would have noticed it. Instead, she adopted an attitude that reassured me and, indeed, made me glad: a quiet, a very quiet irritability of the kind that one feels when a hope and expectation whose fulfilment one had been waiting for so patiently for so long have still not come about, even though one has done everything in one's power to remove any obstacles, whether possible or impossible.

'"I'm not going today," she said one day, and there was irritation in her voice.

'I'm ashamed to say so, and I was ashamed of myself when I went to the cinema to celebrate.

'Two days later she went again and said *Bonsoir* when she came home.

'I felt awkward, and not like a clumsy citizen of Bern but – it was strange, very strange – like an awkward and heavy-handed Dutchman who has somehow, by mistake and undeservedly, had a gleaming daughter from the glittering world of French chateaux, an oversight that has been revealed by Lévy's appearance on the scene. Awkwardly, slowly, I dragged myself through the rooms of the university and made one mistake after another. Secretly, I pronounced my first name in a French accent, and for a while I left out the *j* in my name so that it might pass for a French one.

'Until the tide within me turned. I began to fasten on to the wooden, heavy-handed Dutchman that Lévy's glamour, Lévy's notional glamour, had created within me like a very real counter-fiction. My parents, with their curious, but entirely inconsequential affection for Holland, had given me a second Christian name: Gerrit. My full name is Martijn Gerrit van Vliet. I have always despised it, this pointed, divided name, a name like a whirring saw crunching its way through bursting paint. But now I dredged it out. I signed myself with it and received astonished, questioning glances, which I met with a menacing frown so that no one asked any further questions.

'I dressed as inelegantly as possible, bulging trousers, rumpled jackets, wrinkled shirts, worn-out shoes. And that still wasn't enough. I drove to Amsterdam and played the Dutchman with a few pitiful scraps of Dutch, making a fool of myself more than once. I lay there sleeplessly on the bed, having become alien to Lea and also to myself. I thought of my great-grandfather, the fraudulent banker who had driven hordes of people in this city to their ruin. And I thought often about how I had wanted to become a forger. Often I stood by the bridges over the canals and looked down at the water. But there was no point, they were far too low.

'Lea said nothing, even though I secretly hoped she was able to interpret the signs. Because what was the point of the masquerade if she of all people didn't recognize it for what it was: the attempt to conquer my pain through self-destruction? What was the point if she didn't understand that in my helplessness I had to respond to the imagined affront with self-destructive actions – because a spiritual pain to which one makes one's own contribution is easier to bear than one by which one is simply afflicted?

'During that time there was only Lévy. She lived only in Neuchâtel, in Bern she was merely present, always waiting to run to the station. Suddenly – or at least that was how I imagined it – she uttered the name *Bümpliz* so that it sounded utterly ridiculous, no longer lovingly ridiculous as it had on Cécile's lips, but ridiculous through contempt, contemptible: how could one live in a part of the city with a name like that? Quite impossible. Places worth taking seriously had French names, and above all those names there gleamed a royal name: NEUCHÂTEL. Sometimes I even imagined her on the station platform, waiting for the train to Bern and unhappily calculating how many hours it would be before she could alight from the train here again. Then she seemed to me to be full of the reluctance that was demonstrated by her foot beating an ugly, irregular rhythm on the concrete, the rhythm of longing and annoyance, of impatient waiting and repulsive insignificance assumed by everything on which David's light did not fall.

'Then one day, a good year after St Moritz, a new sound came from her room when I came home.

'My body reacted faster than my mind and I locked myself in the lavatory. He had bought her another violin – it was the only possible interpretation. The instrument that we had bought together in St Gallen was no longer good enough for a pupil of David Lévy. I struggled to work out how the tone differed from the old one, but one hears too little through two doors. I waited until my breath had calmed down, then waited again outside Lea's door, and finally I knocked. That was how we had done things for a long time, and it was fine. Except that Lévy had made the knocking different: I was now asking permission to enter a strange world. And now that the familiar door closed me off from new notes, which came rich and weighty through the wood, I had palpitations, because I felt that something had begun again, something that would drive Lea still further from me.

'Red patches were scattered over Lea's throat, her eyes gleamed feverishly. The violin she was holding was made of surprisingly dark wood. That's all I know. I didn't look any closer, not even secretly; the idea that the traces of his fingers were on it, and that his grease and his sweat were now being transferred to Lea's fingers, too, filled me with nausea. Just his hands. Once when I saw him walking by in an alley in Bern, I dreamed afterwards that he was limping and walking with a stick whose silver handle looked dull, worn and faded from the sour sweat of his wrinkled, old man's hand.

'Lea looked at me uneasily. "It's David's violin. He gave it to me. Nicola Amati made it, in Cremona, in 1653."'

18

THE NEXT THING I remember is Van Vliet's hands on the bed covers. Big, strong hands with fine hairs on the back and strikingly ridged nails. The hands he used to do his experiments, to move his chess pieces. The hands that had once, just once, pressed down on the strings of Lea's violin. The hands which had done something that destroyed his career, so that he now lived in two rooms. The hands he no longer trusted when he saw a lorry approaching.

Between our rooms in the Geneva hotel there was a connecting door to which I paid no attention. Until I heard the sound of the door handle. It must have been a double door, because nothing on my side changed. I waited, and from time to time put my ear to the wood, until I heard Van Vliet's snoring. When it was loud and regular, I quietly opened my side of the door. His was wide open. His clothes were scattered carelessly on the chairs, his shirt was on the floor. He had drunk and told his stories, told his stories and drunk. I was amazed that he had managed to maintain his concentration after all that wine, and then very suddenly he had collapsed and fallen silent. I didn't need to support him, but it took a long time before we were back in our rooms.

Eventually, he had produced the photograph of Lea that he had taken the evening before her first performance at school, when she had made a mistake in Mozart's Rondo. If it had been my daughter – I would have left the picture in my wallet. A slender girl in a simple black dress, with long, dark hair that looked in the coarse resolution of the photograph as if it were run through with gold dust. A bit of lipstick on her full, even lips, which made her look a little like a child-woman. A look that came from grey, perhaps even greenish eyes, mocking, flirtatious and astonishingly confident for an eleven-year-old girl. *A lady waiting for the spotlights to come on.*

One could have fallen in love even with this girl. But how much more violent were the emotions provoked by Lea at eighteen! Van Vliet had hesitated to show me this photograph. He had put the wallet back in his pocket and then taken it back out again. 'That was just before he gave her the violin, that damned Amati.'

She was standing in a spacious corridor that looked like an ample, elegantly decorated flat, leaning against a chest of drawers with a mirror on top, so that past her shoulder you could see the back of her head, with a chignon above her long, slender neck. That knot of hair – I don't know how to explain it: it didn't make her look old or old-fashioned. It had the opposite effect: of making her look like a vulnerable girl, a girl full of order and discipline who wanted to do right by everyone. Not a bluestocking, not just a swot, far from it. This was an elegant young woman in a perfectly cut red dress, and the thin, shining leather belt with the matt gold buckle was the dot on the *i*. The even, full lips were no longer those of a child-woman, they belonged to a real woman, a countess who seemed to be utterly unaware of her aura. In her eyes, which had a hint of pathos about them, there were two things I never thought I would see merging in a single gaze: touching, childish vulnerability and a piercing challenge that chilled the blood. Van Vliet had been right: it wasn't arrogance or superiority, it was a challenge, and one that she was making of herself no less than anyone else. Yes, this was the girl who wanted to hurl her violin into the audience when she made a mistake. And yes, this was the woman who was capable of getting to her feet in the middle of dinner and leaving Marie, her great love from her childhood days, sitting where she was when someone like David Lévy appeared on the scene and promised her a brilliant future in aristocratic French.

Van Vliet had become uneasy when I held the photograph close in front of my eyes to examine every detail of that gaze. He looked at me. He had wanted and yet not wanted me to make myself an image, and now that it was going on too long for me he was starting to rue it. A dangerous spark appeared in his eyes. He was still at hers, he was still in their shared flat, his jealousy could go up at any time like a jet of flame and that was how it would stay.

I handed him the photograph. He gave me a challenging look. Tom Courtenay. I just nodded. Any word could be the wrong one. Now I carefully closed my side of the door. I didn't want him to feel trapped when he woke up. He had left the light on in the bathroom. It fell through the chink in the door and bathed part of the room in diffuse brightness. I thought of something I hadn't thought of for many decades: the *veilleuse*, a night light for children who were afraid of the dark. It was like a light bulb of milky glass, screwed at night into the fixture of the ceiling light by my mother. I saw her hand in front of me, its rotating movement. Trust – that was what that motion meant. Trust that this hand would always be able to take my fear away from me, whatever happened.

I broke that *veilleuse* with an axe. I rummaged in a toolbox in the basement until I found it. I took it, laid it on the wooden block and struck, a dull blow, a crunch and a tinkle, a thousand fragments. An execution. No, not of my mother, but of my own blind trust; no, not just in my mother, not even especially in her, but in everyone and everything. I don't know how to explain it any better.

From then on I trusted only myself. Until the morning I handed Paul the scalpel. A few days later I had a dream: Paul's eyes above the face mask weren't shocked, just boundlessly amazed and glad that we had suddenly come so far. What could I do about the fact, I thought afterwards, that Helen, his wife followed me into the garden when they had guests and I wanted to be alone for a while? Her coming from Boston wasn't a good enough excuse, and Paul knew that too.

Had I ever had friends, I wondered, real friends?

And now? Now, in the next room there lay a man who left the door open and the light on to be able to go to sleep. What would it be like the other way round? What would it be like to trust Martijn van Vliet? He still wore the wedding ring that Cécile had put on his finger. Cécile, who must have known that he didn't want the responsibility of a child.

When Bern and Neuchâtel were covered with snow, he had sometimes driven to the Oberland and hired cross-country skis. He had sought the reassurance that only silence can give. He had wondered who he would be once he was independent of Lea, and how things would continue. Not least professionally. Ruth Adamek had effectively taken over the research project long ago. He just signed the papers. She was standing behind him when he had wanted to know more about what was going on and had started flicking. 'Sign it!' she had snapped. Then he tore up the application. She grinned.

After that he had tried for the last time. Tablets. Lie down and sleep. Be snowed in. As if he'd never existed. Then at the last moment the thought of Lea. That she needed him, in spite of Lévy. One day perhaps because of Lévy.

I couldn't get to sleep. I had to prevent it. I felt as if my own life depended on it.

Suddenly I wished I could turn back time to before the morning in Saint-Rémy with the girl on the back seat of the rattling Vespa. It had been lovely, in those rural inns with Somerset Maugham in a dim light.

I couldn't call Leslie at four in the morning. And what would I have said?

I went to the lobby and strolled through the hotel arcade with the shop windows. I knew the hotel, but I'd never been here at the back. Eventually I discovered a library. I turned on the light and stepped in. Metres of Simenon, city guides, Stephen King, a book about Napoleon, a selection of Apollinaire, poems by Robert Frost. *Leaves of Grass*, the book that had flourished inside Walt Whitman for a lifetime. *I cannot be awake, for nothing looks to me as it did before, / Or else I am awake for the first time, and all before has been / a mean sleep.* An intense hunger flowed through me, a hunger for Whitman. I sat down in an armchair until it was light outside. I read with my tongue. I wanted to live, live, live.

19

DAVID LÉVY turned Lea into Mademoiselle Bach. MADEMOISELLE BACH. The papers published those two words again and again, first towards the back of the paper and in small letters, then the letters got bigger and the articles longer; there were pictures, too, and they too got bigger and bigger; in the end her face above the violin appeared on the front pages of the tabloids. For Van Vliet this all felt like a slow-motion, halting zoom; there was something doom-laden about its inexorability. He wanted to know if I'd seen any of that. 'I don't read the papers,' I said. 'I'm not interested in what journalists think.' I just want the facts, as dry as agency reports. I know what I'm supposed to think about it. It may sound strange, because he had already told me all these things from his life, but that was the first time I had the feeling that he liked me. Not just his audience. Me.

The first performances came a few weeks after Lévy had given her his violin. He still had some influence in the music world, it turned out. Neuchâtel, Biel, Lausanne. Amazement about the young girl who played the music of Johann Sebastian Bach with a clarity that enchanted everyone and which filled the increasingly packed halls with a sound whose like had not been heard for ages. The journalists wrote about an unheard-of *energy* in her playing, and once Van Vliet also read the word that had run through his head in St Moritz: *sacred.*

He read everything; the cardboard box of newspaper cuttings filled up. He looked at every photograph and studied it for a long time. Lea's bows because more confident, more lady-like, more routine, her smile firmer, more dependable, more keenly etched. His daughter was becoming increasingly alien to him.

'I was glad when she came out with another of her strange sentences – as a memory of the fact that behind the façade of Mademoiselle Bach there was still my daughter, the girl I had stood in the station with ten years before, listening to Loyola de Colón.'

But now fear sometimes crept in, real fear, and it became more frequent, more compelling. Because there were days when Lea's sentences were more off-kilter than usual. 'I told the technician it was too dark in the hall, much too dark; it would be nicer if I had to make out every individual face in the audience.' 'Just imagine, my driving teacher asked me if it was a violin or a viola. He doesn't even know there's a difference. And he listens to opera all day, particularly that new bass baritone from Peru.' 'Davíd was, as always, right about the recording contract: why does he always forget that I can't stand smoke? No one in the company is even interested.' On days like that her father felt as if it wasn't only his daughter's language that was off-kilter, it was her mind. He read books about it and took care to ensure that Lea didn't see them.

It wouldn't have been necessary. She no longer seemed even slightly interested in what her father did. He was so inconsolable about this that he started smoking in the sitting room in the hope that she would at least protest. Nothing. He stopped again and had the whole flat cleaned. No word about that from Lea either. He travelled, went to a conference again and stayed a few days, to forget Marie with another woman. 'You were away for a long time,' Lea said. Had she spent the night in Neuchâtel? *He's not that kind of man.*

Van Vliet was summoned by the headmaster of Lea's school. The leaving exam was in six months. It didn't look good for Lea. She was fine in the subjects that called for intelligence most of all. The outlook was catastrophic for the ones that everyone had to cram for. And she was missing a lot, far too much. The headmaster was understanding, generous. Of course he was proud of Mademoiselle Bach, the whole school was proud. But he couldn't ignore all the rules of the school. Please would her father have a word with her, please?

If only Marie had still been there. But Marie had ceased to exist two years ago. She had frozen when Van Vliet had asked, after the concert in St Moritz, whether she wouldn't call in; talk, not apologize, just talk.

From Marie to Lévy: a violent tectonic shift must have taken place inside Lea. He would have loved to understand. Was he simply not the man to understand something like that? Would Cécile have understood, that worldly woman who often laughed at his naiveté?

He tried to talk to Katharina Walther about it. *Marie Pasteur. Yes, yes, Marie Pasteur.* He hadn't forgotten her words, which was why he had hesitated. She immediately switched to Lévy's side. A natural substitution process. A normalization. And the man was a brilliant teacher!

A normalization. Van Vliet had to think about that later on, when he was sitting opposite the Maghrebi and had to endure his X-ray gaze.

Marie had ceased to exist. Should he get over himself and talk to Lévy? '*Oui?*' Lévy said at the other end of the line. '*Votre jeu: sublime,*' Van Vliet heard the voice saying. He put down the phone.

He talked with Lea. Or rather: to her. He sat down in the armchair in her room, as he hadn't done for ages. He told her about his conversation with the headmaster, about his good intentions and his concern. He admonished, threatened, pleaded. Above all, I think, he pleaded. He pleaded with her to do her school leaving exam. To take a break from the performances and recover. With him, if she wanted.

It worked, at least temporarily. She spent more time at home, they ate together more often. Van Vliet found himself hoping that he would be close to her once again. Only a few weeks until the exams. A big performance was scheduled in Geneva two days after the last exams. Orchestre de la Suisse Romande, Bach's E major Concerto. Instead of collecting her marks, she would be sitting on the train to Geneva to be in time for the rehearsals.

While being quizzed about dates and chemical compounds her face suddenly went blank and she said nothing more. Van Vliet was worried about her brain. But she wasn't having a brainstorm, she was just thinking all of a sudden about Geneva and the famous conductor that she didn't want to disappoint. He saw the fear in her empty eyes, and again he cursed her fame, and he cursed Joe, the music teacher who had put her forward for St Moritz.

And then came the day when Van Vliet turned into Jean-Louis Trintignant, whom he had seen, while sitting next to Cécile, driving through the night behind the wheel of his filthy racing car, dashing from the Côte d'Azur to Paris. But Trintignant, in my imagination, had the face of Tom Courtenay. He smoked like a chimney; the smoke obscured his vision; his eyes stung, and he had, I think, a splitting headache, while he rushed from Bern to Ins and on to Neuchâtel, cutting corners, screeching tyres, flashing lights and cursing; and always that time in front of his eyes: 12.00, Lea's Biology exam. He had to pick her up and bring her back, with any luck he'd just make it. The exam timetable had been on the kitchen table. He had pounced on it, then the white-hot certainty that Lea had got her days mixed up and gone to

Neuchâtel, because the violin wasn't there. At Ins Station he had just missed the train on which she must have been, so on to Neuchâtel. Once he took the wrong fork in the road and had to turn round; no car park at Neuchâtel; taxi drivers cursing when he pulled in alongside them, but not for long, because the train had arrived a few minutes previously; LÉVY DAVID, frantically flicking through the phone book; he asked the taxi drivers to tell him the way, idiotic grins and shaking of heads; he ran a red light; after a bit of time spent aimlessly driving back and forth, a policeman who was able to tell the way. Shortly afterwards he saw her with her violin case over her shoulder.

She was confused, stubborn, didn't believe it, didn't want to. At least to tell her briefly. She ran the doorbell of the dark house. Lévy in his dressing gown, fully dressed underneath, and still: dressing gown, *Je me suis trompée, je suis désolée*, he half heard it, half read it on her lips, her apologetic expression, servile, he thought, her hand gestures in his direction. Lévy's expression, not a sign of recognition, not a greeting. The violin case got caught in the car door, a reproachful look as if it were all his fault. Gregor Mendel, Charles Darwin, DNA, nucleases, nucleoles, nucleotide; she had to hold on in the bends; the clock on the dashboard ticked the minutes away, and then, all of a sudden, she went to pieces and wept, her shoulders twitched, she bent low until her head hung between her knees.

He stopped on the corner outside the school and took her in his arms. For precious minutes he held his child, who sobbed out her fear in hard, irregular bursts, her fear of the exam, of Geneva, of the damp hands, of Lévy's judgement and of being lonely in the hotel room. Van Vliet wiped his eyes as he told me about it.

She had slowly calmed down. He had wiped away her tears, stroked her hair smooth and kissed her on the forehead. 'You're Lea Van Vliet,' he had said. She had smiled like a castaway. On the corner she had waved.

A few streets on, in a quiet car park, Van Vliet himself had gone to pieces. He closed the window so that no one could hear him sobbing. With a loud, animal groan everything had collapsed around him: his fear for Lea, his homesickness for former times, his own loneliness, his jealousy and hatred of the man in the dressing gown who had bound her to him with a violin by Nicola Amati. He opened the violin case and for one crazed, insane moment he considered putting the instrument down in front of the wheels and driving over it. Before driving to the Oberland and lying down under the snow.

After that there was no time to drive home. He washed his face in a fountain and collected Lea. She had passed, although without distinction. She threw her arms around his neck. She must have felt what was left of the damp from the fountain and looked at him. 'You've been crying,' she said.

They drove to the Rosengarten to eat. He had hoped it would be a meal over which they could talk about her emotions, which had spilled from beneath her tears. But when they had ordered, Lea picked up the phone and called Lévy. 'Just very quickly,' she said, apologetically. '*Je suis désolée, je me suis trompée de jour . . . Non, l'oral . . . Oui, réussi . . . Non, pas très bien . . . Oui, à trés bientôt.' À bientôt* hadn't been enough, it had had to be *à très bientôt*. That ugly little word had destroyed everything. When Van Vliet talked about it, it was as if he were hearing the wretched syllable at that very moment. He had left his dinner half-eaten and they had driven home in silence. The hard shell had closed over their feelings once more, for both of them.

Once again he braced himself, picked her up after the last exam and drove her to Geneva. He drove to the concert as well. He walked through the city and saw the posters: LEA VAN VLIET. He had learned to love and hate such posters. Sometimes he had run his hand over the smooth, shiny paper. Then again, when he thought he was unobserved, he had torn it into tiny pieces, vandalism against his daughter's fame. Once a policeman had seen him do it and apprehended him. 'I'm the father,' he had said and shown him his ID. The policeman had looked at him in admiration. 'What's it like to have such a famous daughter?' 'Difficult,' Van Vliet had replied. The policeman had laughed. As he walked on Van Vliet had been annoyed that the matter had turned into a joke like that and had spat on the ground. The policeman, who had stopped, had seen it. For a moment their eyes locked like the eyes of enemies. At least that was how it had seemed to Van Vliet.

He hadn't been to one of Lea's concerts for a long time. Seeing Lévy's salt-and-pepper mane in the auditorium was unbearable. Even now it was unbearable. But then he managed to forget it. Because his daughter was playing as he had never heard her play before. St Moritz was nothing in comparison. But then he had thought: A cathedral of notes. But that had been a little church compared with the cathedral that she built with her Amati notes over the whole city of Geneva and all the water. For her father nothing existed but this cathedral of clarity and night-black blue, translated into sound. And there was also the source of that monumental sacred architecture: Lea's hands which, as sure as Marie's hands, drew sounds from that incomparable instrument that Nicola Amati had made in 1653. And her face above the chin-rest, her eyes mostly closed. Since that evening in St Moritz when David Lévy had come to their table as if out of nowhere, she had never again used a white cloth for her chin. The colour was now mauve, as Lea called it. He had investigated the cloths and found what he was looking for: LUC BLANC, NEUCHÂTEL, the company name in tiny black letters. Now, once again, Lea pressed her chin to such a cloth. The muscles of her face followed the music, both the line of the melody and the curve of the technical difficulties. He thought of how that face had dissolved a few days before and had been pressed wetly against his cheek. *À très bientôt.* Lévy sat motionlessly on his seat in the front row.

He was the one on whom she bestowed her first glance before she bowed. The glance of the grateful, proud and, yes, loving student. The conductor mimed a kiss of her hand. She shook the lead violinist's hand. Only in the car did Van Vliet know what had disturbed him about it: the gesture had been unpredictable, terribly unpredictable. He had felt as if Lea had been caught up in an enormous clockwork mechanism, the gigantic, grinding wheels of the concert business, and now she was performing all the movements that the predetermined ballistic curves dictated. The father thought of the way she had bowed at her first performance in the school. Although graceful, there had been something shy about it, a shyness that was missing now; it had made way for the glamour of the star.

Lévy got to Lea before her father did. They both walked up to him. '*David, je vous présente mon père*,' Lea said to the man who had turned Neuchâtel into a hated fortress. Lévy's face was at ease, detached. The two unequal men shook hands. Lévy's hand was cold, anaemic.

'*Sublime, n'est-ce pas?*' he said.

'*Divin, celeste*,' Van Vliet said.

He had looked up the words long ago to be ready if he met his daughter's sublime, heavenly teacher. When he asked a French school friend for advice, she had laughed. 'It drips with irony,' she had said, 'especially *céleste*. My God, *céleste* in an exchange like that! *Sublime!*'

Every now and again he had dreamed of that encounter, and then the words hadn't come to mind. Now they came. In Lea's face rage about her father's irony mingled with pride at his quickness of mind, and a linguistic knowledge she hadn't known he possessed. 'There's a party now,' she said hesitantly. 'David is taking me in his car. He has to go to Bern anyway.'

David, but still *vous*, Van Vliet had thought in the car. He felt Lévy's cold hand, which he had had to touch once more when saying goodbye. Lea hadn't asked if he wanted to come to the party as well. Of course, he wouldn't have gone. But he didn't want to be excluded, either, not even by Lea, particularly not by her. He thought of the Roe garden and the movement with which she had picked up the telephone. It had been a movement like a wall, and the wall had grown with each passing second in which she had waited with anticipation for Lévy to speak in a melodious voice. Now he had lost again and she would be sitting beside Lévy in the green Jaguar in the middle of the night.

Van Vliet didn't say it, but we both knew that he had been thinking of Marie's hand slicing open the whole length of a green Jaguar with the pointed key.

I see you dashing to Ins and Neuchâtel, Martijn, your daughter and one goal in front of your eyes. And I see you driving at night from Geneva to Bern, without a wife, without a speed, without a goal. A little like Tom Courtenay when he had to return to the treadmill of harassment, a victor for a matter of minutes, a loser for years.

20

WHEN HE GOT HOME, Van Vliet had taken a sleeping pill. He didn't want to hear Lea coming home. The next morning she laid the breakfast table for two. It was the first time he had refused a peace offering from his daughter. He drank a cup of coffee standing up.

'I'm going away for a few days,' he said.

Lea looked anxious. As if her indifference over the previous few months had not existed.

'For how long?'

'No idea.'

Her eyes wavered. 'Alone?'

Van Vliet refused to answer. First time for that, too. Her expression had said: *Marie*. She must have sensed it. She had never said anything. But she must have sensed it. Marie had become taboo, a crystallization point of woundedness, guilt and embarrassment. He would never have thought that there could be a taboo between him and his daughter. When she had, back then, in the railway station, after Loyola's playing, resisted his protective movement – that had been the awakening of a will of her own; it had hurt, but he had learned to understand, accept and in the end encourage it. Like the other kinds of independence that had developed since then. But that forbidden zone around Marie, that ice age of silence and denial: it tore him apart that things had come to this between them.

'So, I'm off,' he said in parting. He was sure, quite sure, that she knew: he was quoting the ritual words she uttered when she set off for Neuchâtel. She looked lost, standing there in the corridor: a girl who would shortly find her school leaving certificate in the letter box; a star whose name was on every wall and in all the newspapers; a violin student who loved her teacher, even if she was never allowed to stay overnight. Van Vliet froze when he saw how lost she was. He was inches away from closing the door again and sitting down at the breakfast table. But that thing about the party the previous evening had been one thing too many. He left.

He had told me all of this over breakfast. He had knocked at the door of my room, not the connecting door. He had to knock for a long time. It had been almost eight when I had fallen asleep with lines from Walt Whitman running through my mind. Breakfast time was over, but we persuaded the waitress. And now we were sitting in our coats by the lake, ready to travel and yet not ready. He didn't want to go to his two silent rooms, and I was afraid of Bern. How would it be? Would we simply say goodbye outside my house, and he would drive to his place, along the roads of Bern, down which no lorries thundered at this time of night? What would I do with his unhappiness? What would he do with the knowledge that I knew of it? An intimacy of that magnitude, suddenly being parted: wasn't it something terrible, barbaric? Something simply impossible? But what else?

And so we sat there, shivering, watching the swans, and Van Vliet told me how he had got back on his feet.

'After that long time I got back on my feet. As I did so I realized how small I had allowed Ruth Adamek to make me. At first I sat in the office with my suitcase and looked at my desk, which was becoming increasingly empty: because I was there so rarely, they simply took my tasks away from me and did them themselves. I no longer had any idea what was happening in my institute.' He flicked his cigarette butt in the lake. 'When I finally grasped that, up there, looking at the mountains, I didn't feel so bad. At any rate I persuaded myself. Forging money, freedom, recklessness, just letting things rush by – why not? But it wasn't the truth. In fact, I sense that my dignity was in danger. Big word, dramatic word. I would never have thought I'd have to strive for it one day. But it was the right word. Perhaps not least because of the evening in Geneva. I don't know. The empty desk wasn't funny any more. I left.'

He didn't go to the Oberland. He took the train to Milan.

'I didn't have suitable clothes for the opera. I don't have any, in fact. But on the second evening someone showed up and offered me a ticket for La Scala. *Idomeneo*. I was ripped off, more than that. So two days after Lea's concert I sat in shabby clothes at the opera house in Milan and studied the violinists in the orchestra pit. I imagined Lea there. And somehow that was the spark: she would study music at the Conservatoire; she was now my grown-up daughter who made her money with concerts and records, and the important thing now was to let her go; eventually Lévy would be a thing of the past as well; a flat of her own, a responsibility of her own, freedom, freedom for both of us. After that *Idomeneo* was my opera. I had no idea what happened in it and what it sounded like, but it was a wonderful opera, the opera of my liberation from responsibility, which Cécile had lumbered me with, and which had almost left me in pieces.

'The problem was just: I didn't believe a word of what I said. But I refused to see it, so I worked on that self-betrayal with all the new energy I persuaded myself I had.

'But first I allowed myself a few days in Northern Italian cities and by Lake Garda. A father who had finally found the correct attitude towards his adult daughter. A man who was at the start of a new phase of his life, full of new freedom. Glances from women, even young ones. A new suitcase.

'And then that book about violin-making in Cremona. Amati, Stradivarius, the Guarneris. I still remember: I didn't feel quite at ease when I was standing by the till. As if the tide of a menacing, treacherous future were surging towards me. As if the book showed me something, a whirlpool in which I would disappear. But I didn't want to know anything about that feeling. I would bring the book to Lea: a gesture of reconciliation, a generous gesture, which, through Amati, also included Lévy.

'After I got back I resumed my job, so to speak. I got to the office earlier than anyone else and left later. I asked them to bring me all the documents from the last few months. I asked them to describe the results of the experiments that we had been given money for, and asked about the details of the new projects. I was quiet and concise. They were afraid of my energy and my concentration, which they had almost forgotten. Because mistakes came to light: incorrect calculations, incorrect estimates, the wrong questions. The contracts of two colleagues were to be extended. I refused to sign. When I discovered that Ruth Adamek had signed them in my place, I called HR and cancelled them. I called Ruth in, and read her the riot act. She was about to protest, but that was just the start. "Not now!" I said when someone tried to come in. I must have said it so piercingly that she blanched. I pulled over a stack of papers that I had worked on through the night. She recognized the stack and gasped. I listed her bad decisions, one after another. She tried to blame me, to blame my constant absence. I interrupted her. I looked at her and felt her breath on the back of my neck, the time she had snapped, 'Sign!' I saw her grinning after I had torn up the application. I read out the miscalculations, the false premises, the incorrect interpretations of the data.

I read them out, one after another. I repeated them. I chanted them. I destroyed Ruth Adamek, who had never forgiven me for not falling for her miniskirt. An icy wind swept down the corridors. I relished it.

'And that wasn't enough. I staged a coup within the industry and acquired research money in the tens of millions. When I left the committee meeting I had to hold on to something in the lift. My insouciance had stung, I had seen it in their faces, and she had raised the stakes again. It wasn't a scam, but the whole thing was risky, to put it mildly.

'I was summoned to see the vice chancellor. He congratulated me on the acquisition. "Child's play," I said, "and entirely without significance. My research, I mean. No use to anyone. It might just as well be forgotten about." He got over the shock very quickly, I must give him that, and laughed loudly. "I didn't know you were such a joker!" My face was deadly serious. "It's not a joke, I'm perfectly serious." And then I tried something I'd once seen a comedian do: I suddenly started roaring with laughter, so that my deadly serious face looked like an elaborate prelude to that laughter, it just burst out of me, and then the vice chancellor started laughing, too. I cranked myself up and roared, until he roared too; the roaring sounded as if it must be audible all over the university. I cranked it up still further, because now I thought the roaring was completely hilarious. I laughed till the tears came and in the end the vice chancellor took out his handkerchief as well. "Van Vliet," he said, "you're a marvel. All Dutchmen are marvels." It was so silly, so completely idiotic, that I burst out laughing all over again, and now our roaring competition went into the third round. By way of farewell, he enquired after Mademoiselle Mozart. "Bach," I said. "Johann Sebastian Bach." "That's what I said," he said and clapped me on the shoulder.

'How very different our next meeting would be!'

21

On 5 January Lea turned twenty. Three days later Lévy told her he would shortly get married and go travelling with his wife for some time. That was the beginning of the disaster.

There had been harbingers of what was to come. Normally, he had worked with Lea even between Christmas and the New Year, and after New Year things continued as before. This time there was a break between the years. Van Vliet didn't ask; he was just gratefully aware of it. There were Christmas decorations in the flat once more, and Lea helped. But her mind wasn't on it. And what alarmed her father: she didn't play her instrument, not a note. Slept till midday, sat around. He gave her the book about the Cremona school of violin-making, which he had bought on his way to Milan. It lay unopened on the table for a few days, then she began to flick through it.

First she read everything about Nicola Amati, whose hands had made her violin. The colour returned to her face. Van Vliet sensed it: she was constantly thinking about Lévy, Nicola Amati was only a substitute. 'He was the one who changed the pointed *gamba* shape to the shape it has today,' she said. Her father sat down beside her at the kitchen table and together they read everything about the measurements of a violin body, the lacquer, the strength of the wood used for the individual parts, the shape of the *f*-holes and the scroll. The instrument over in the music room was a *large Amati model*, she hadn't known the term before. Neither had she known that such violins were known, because of their sound, as *Mozart violins*. Her cheeks began to glow, a few red patches appeared on her throat. With every new detail Neuchâtel edged closer. It pained her father, but he sat where he was, and then they went through the Amati dynasty's family tree together.

GUARNERI DEL GESÙ. There at the kitchen table, during the last days of the year, Van Vliet didn't guess what misfortune awaited her behind that name. What doom it would lead to for both of them. At first it was just the name that gripped Lea and distracted her attention from Amati and Lévy. Suddenly in her eyes and her voice there appeared a fresh and innocent curiosity which was not darting sidelong glances at Neuchâtel. They got to know that family tree as well. Andrea, the grandfather; Giuseppe Giovanni, who would later be nicknamed *filius Andreae*; and his son Bartolomeo Giuseppe, who identified himself on his violin labels as *Joseph Guarnerius*. He added a cross as well as the letters HIS, which might have meant IN HOC SIGNO or IESUS HOMINUM SALVATOR. That was why he was later known as *Guarneri del Gesù*. Lea liked that nickname; she liked it so much that Van Vliet thought of the cross that Marie used to draw on her forehead. For one brief, dangerous moment he was tempted to ask her about it. Luckily, Lea had just read something that put her in a state of cheerful excitement.

'Look, Dad, Niccolò had a Guarneri del Gesù as well! It's called *Il Cannone*. He left it to the city of Genoa. You can see it in the city hall there. Couldn't we go?'

Van Vliet bought the airline tickets that day, and booked the hotel. They would spend Lea's birthday in Genoa, in front of the case containing Paganini's violin. What could be more appropriate? It was the perfect present for that birthday. And much more importantly: it was the first journey in many years that he would take with his daughter, just with her. The last one had been interrupted, because Lea wanted to get back to Marie. This one, her father swore, would not be interrupted; if necessary Lea's phone would get lost on the way. He was delighted, he was so delighted, that he bought Lea a luxury suitcase, the most expensive one in the shop, and he also brought along an enormous book full of pictures of Genoa and a map of the city. Starting the New Year in Genoa with his daughter: really, it was bound to be a year in which things would take a turn for the better in other respects as well. He hadn't felt so confident in years.

But all of a sudden Lea didn't want to go. Instead she wanted to see that exhibition in Neuchâtel that she'd read about in the paper. Van Vliet looked at the new suitcase. The whole thing was like a dream that vanishes in the morning light. 'I don't think I've ever been so disappointed,' he said. 'It was as if I'd run into invisible armoured glass, my whole face hurt.' He cancelled the hotel room and tore up the flight tickets. On Lea's birthday he went to the institute early and stayed at his computer until the small hours. For the first time he thought of moving to a different flat.

Three days later she came back from Neuchâtel without her violin. She had been caught in the rain, her hair hung in her face in rat's tails. But that wasn't what made him shudder. It was the look on her face.

'A crazed look. Yes, that's the only word for it: crazed. A look that testified to a terrible inner disorder. It told me she had lost her mental equilibrium completely, and was drifting along on a flood of injury. The worst moment was when that look brushed against me. "Oh, you're here, too," it seemed to say. "Why, in fact, you can't help me, not you, you're the last one who could." She crept under the covers in her wet clothes. She didn't even take off her shoes. When I opened the door a crack she was sobbing into her pillow.'

Van Vliet sat down at the kitchen table and waited. He tried to prepare himself, to get his feelings in order. A break so intense that she had given him back the violin. He tried to be honest with himself. The relief was undeniable. So that was over. But what now? Was that also the end of her career, of her life as a musician? People would see and above all hear that she was no longer playing the Amati. The violin from St

Gallen no longer filled concert halls. And apart from that: who would organize the concerts for her now?

He forgot to hide the sleeping pills. Lea found them, but there weren't many left in the pack. When he noticed, he woke her, made coffee and walked up and down with her all through the flat. The medication had broken down the barriers of censorship, and now it came exploding out of her, crude, raw and incoherent. Lévy had introduced her to his bride. 'Tits and arse!' Lea yelled thickly. It was hard for Van Vliet to repeat the words to me. He had hesitated and clearly much else besides had exploded out of Lea. The father, who had grown up in the alleys, was disturbed to hear how vulgar his divine daughter could be. He realized: he had imagined her as a fairy, a fairy by nature, to whom everything foul and ordinary was entirely alien. And something else disturbed him, something that had already bothered him at the concert in Geneva when she had shaken hands with the leader: that she was doing things that were so precisely predictable. Because her coarse insults, with the ever-recurring word *putain*, were as schematic and predictable as the orgies of jealousy in a soap opera. After the high-speed drive from Neuchâtel to Bern he had enjoyed holding his weeping daughter in his arms. Now, when he had to drag her through the flat, for the first time since she was born he felt a revulsion at the touch of her sleepy body, from which all these scurrilous and predictable things were spilling.

I thought about the time when I first heard Leslie saying *shit* and *bitch*. We were watching television and even I flinched. '*Growing up*,' said Joanne and smiled.

'Most of the things we say are predictable,' I said.

Van Vliet took a drag on his cigarette and looked out at the lake. 'Could be,' he said. 'Perhaps it's inevitable. That they should say things that some drunk scriptwriter could have put in their mouths – it was terrible, absolutely revolting. It was as if I were dragging some random young girl through the flat, not Lea at all. There had already been so much strangeness between us. So why not that, too?'

Years later, when Lea was already in the hospice at Saint-Rémy and in the care of the Maghrebi, Van Vliet rang Lévy and asked for a meeting. He flinched when he heard the '*Oui?*' of the melodious voice, just as he had the first time he had called him. But this time he went on, and then he drove to Neuchâtel. Lévy and his beautiful young wife, whose paintings hung on the walls and who didn't resemble his wife in the slightest, that wife of whom Lea had spoken in her pill-drunk voice, talked about the dramatic moment when Lea had almost destroyed a million dollars. She had been holding the Amati violin when Lévy introduced his fiancée to her.

'Her eyes . . . I must have sensed it,' Lévy said, 'because I took a few steps towards her. And I was just able to grab her wrist before she could hurl the violin away. It was the last, the very last moment. She let go of the violin and I managed to take hold of the instrument with my other hand. It's worth more than all of this,' and his hand gesture took in the whole of the house.

On the way back Van Vliet thought about how his little Lea had wanted to sling the violin into the audience after that mistake. He also thought about the CD by Dinu Lipatti that she had thrown out of the window, and whose cover had made such an appalling clatter on the tarmac. But for now his task was to take each day as it came. The important thing was to administer the millions that he had freed up with his coup. Right now he couldn't afford to stay away. Ruth Adamek would use every opportunity to take her revenge. Several times a day he phoned home to check that Lea wasn't doing anything stupid. His headaches at work became more intense.

One early morning he waited outside Krompholz to talk to Katharina Walther before the first customers arrived. Much time had passed. He had been cross with her for a long time for talking about Lea's switch from Marie to Lévy as if something morbid were coming to an end. She had followed Mademoiselle Bach's career in the press and had also attended her concerts. She had seen the Geneva concert on television. It came out of the blue when Van Vliet told her about Lea's breakdown.

'She's twenty,' she said after a while. 'She'll get over it. And concerts: there won't be any for a while. The rest will do her good. Other concert agents will get in touch.'

Van Vliet was disappointed. What had he expected? What could he expect when he said nothing about the most important thing?

The most important thing was that Lea's thoughts were slipping. It wasn't just her feelings that were in uproar. It was as if an undertow were coming from the depths of her confused emotions to drag her thinking into the darkness.

There were days when things seemed to have settled down again. But the price of that was the denial of time. Then Lea talked about Neuchâtel and Lévy as if everything was as it had been before. Without noticing that it didn't match the fact that she didn't go there any more and Amati wasn't there. She came home with new clothes that she had bought for imaginary concerts. They were clothes covered with glitter that made her look sluttish and would have been completely out of place in a concert hall. Then she walked around the flat in a little blouse that made her father blush, with blotches of lipstick that made her mouth look swollen. She read the newspaper from the day before yesterday and didn't notice. She rarely knew what day of the week it was. She muddled *Idomeneo* with *Fidelio*, Chechnya and the Czech Republic. She took up smoking even in the flat, but couldn't take the smoke and coughed all the time. 'I saw Caroline in town today. You can't forget everything,' she said. 'Joe has retired, now he's reached his goal. He always liked teaching so much.' And 'Mozart was always very strict with his tempi. It wasn't all that important to him. The notes just came too strictly for him to pay attention to their speed.'

Van Vliet often stayed at the institute until the small hours. There he could rest his head on the table and let the tears come pouring out.

I asked if he had ever thought of a psychiatrist. Of course. But he hadn't known how to broach the idea without her going through the roof. And he had been too ashamed, I thought.

Ashamed? Was that the right expression? He couldn't bear anyone learning of the misfortune that connected him with his daughter. Someone sticking his nose into it. Even if it was a doctor. And besides: how could a stranger have understood something about his daughter that he, her father, didn't understand? He, who knew her off by heart, like the back of his hand, because he had seen her every day for twenty years and knew every fork in the road, every junction, every bend in her life story?

But basically it was this one thing: he didn't want the *alien gaze*, the revealing gaze of another. He would have found it utterly destructive, destructive for Lea and for himself. Yes, not least for himself. The way he experienced the gaze of the Maghrebi, the black, Arab gaze, which, in his hatred, he wished he could push back into those dark eyes, right to the back, until it was extinguished.

There was also the fact that he managed to do something that reinforced his conviction that he and Lea could overcome the crisis all by themselves. One day he saw a little girl having her hand and face licked by a dog. Then he remembered the affection that Lea had experienced from animals in the past. He went with her to the animal home. By that evening they were feeding the new dog.

She immediately clung to the animal, a black giant schnauzer, and it calmed her down; sometimes she seemed almost relaxed. She was tender towards the creature, and when her father saw her like that, he could almost forget the violence and cruelty that were also within her. It was only if a stranger came too close to the dog that it flared up. Then her gaze had a piercing sharpness.

She loved the dog and protected it. Her father became calmer; the danger of pills was past; the dog wouldn't leave her in the lurch. But slowly and imperceptibly a new danger arose: the protector became a child who sought refuge in the dog as she might have done in a human being. Rather than bending down to him or squatting to stroke him, Lea sat beside him on the floor, heedless of the dirt, pressed her head to his and wrapped her arms around him. Van Vliet didn't at first think anything of it; the relief of knowing she was safe took precedence. Although there was sometimes a sad kind of comedy about it when the dog wriggled away because it couldn't breathe or simply because it felt oppressed.

'Nikki,' she would say with a mixture of disappointment and irritation, 'why won't you stay with me?'

It was the name the dog was familiar with from before. In her father's presence she never called it anything else. But one day when Van Vliet was passing by her door he heard her through the open crack calling him *Nicola* or *Niccolò*, the two names flowed into one another. It was like a power surge. Back in his office he tried to calm himself down, to think clearly. Why not see it simply as harmless, funny word play? But in that case why was it secret? *What* was secret? And even if it were a bit more than that and she was somehow connecting the dog – out of some vague and confused feeling – with Amati and Paganini: was that really cause for concern? She was a little wound up and flustered, but not insane.

Van Vliet concentrated on his work. Until suddenly the fear welled up in him like a fountain. '*What if she was?* What if her apparently harmless way of playing around with names heralded an impulse of mental confusion which shifted everything within her like a tectonic tremor?

In one of those moments when he was inundated with panic, Ruth Adamek must have come into his office. She must have been wearing her white lab coat and holding a bunch of keys. Then something must have happened to Van Vliet, something that I read more in his feverish gaze and his rough voice than in his words, which were bare and halting: his assistant, whom he had recently – as he put it – destroyed, appeared to him like the ruthless, peremptory warder in a closed psychiatric unit. And when I say *appeared*, I mean that she was like an apparition, a diabolical epiphany who planned to put him and his daughter behind the hollow, gloomy walls of an institution.

Van Vliet threw her out and became almost violent. The slam of the office door was audible all over the building. If there had been, somewhere within him, in some hidden room that no one knew about, a willingness to seek advice from a psychiatrist: from now on that room was sealed for ever.

'A madhouse. A *madhouse*. I'm not putting Lea in a *madhouse*.'

We had walked for a while and now we were standing again on the shores of Lake Geneva. The brutal word was like a knife with which he cut himself, once, twice, three times. I thought about his words, when he told me about Amsterdam, about the bridges over the canals, the bridges that were too low, and the disguise with the old clothes that he put on to ward off, to defend himself, as clodhopping Dutchman Martijn Gerrit van Vliet, against the glittering David Lévy: *because a spiritual pain to which we ourselves contribute is easier to bear than pain merely inflicted on us.*

'I'm not putting Lea in a madhouse.' He was speaking in the present tense. A terrible present tense. Not just because it denied Lea's death, but also because a helpless, icy fury vibrated in it, a rage against the Maghrebi who had refused him access to his daughter, and whose existence he was able to bear only because it was simply erased by the tense he had used. No, white coats, keys and sealed asylum doors were out of the question.

Not even when Lea had a complete collapse after visiting Marie. Van Vliet had seen her in the distance, her old violin hanging over her shoulder, Nikki on the leash. His stomach tightened. *Marie.* It became a certainty when she boarded the tram. Van Vliet ran to the taxi rank and followed her. The way one follows a sleepwalker to protect her and keep her from falling.

He was hiding in a house doorway on the other side of the street when Lea walked, hesitantly and with her head lowered, towards Marie's house. It was starting to get dark and he saw straight away: there was no light behind Marie's windows. Lea paused, seemed for a moment to want to turn around, and then rang, after all. Nothing. She stroked the dog, waited, rang again. Van Vliet sighed with relief: it had gone well once again. But even though the dog tugged on the lead, Lea didn't go away, but took the violin off her shoulder and sat down on the steps in front of the door. Now father and daughter waited in the falling darkness, speechless and separated by the evening traffic, in which Marie would eventually have to appear.

Should he have gone to her and brought her home? Reminded her that Marie was scared of dogs? If she hadn't had the violin with her, yes, he might have done. But the violin meant: she didn't just want to talk to Marie, she wanted a lesson, and that meant: she wanted to turn back time, she wanted everything to be as it had been before. No trip to St Moritz, no break-up, no David Lévy, no Neuchâtel, she wanted to get back to Mari's batik dresses and all the chintz she had once wanted to bathe in. Van Vliet sensed: over there, on the steps, Lea was suspended above an abyss. She was staggering through time, or rather she no longer knew time, there *was* no time in her any more – there was just that one desire: for things with Marie to be good again, with the woman she had given the gold ring to, had sent all those cards to from Rome, the woman who had drawn a cross on her forehead before every performance.

And her father didn't want to be the one to trample that hope and that longing, and whom she would hate afterwards.

It was already after nine o'clock and black night when Marie parked outside the house. Van Vliet stared across until tears came to his eyes. The dog humped up and tugged on the leash. Marie recoiled, bridled, froze. Now Lea was standing facing her. Van Vliet was glad it was too dark to make out the expression on her face. But perhaps it was even worse having to imagine that expression: a pleading, begging expression on the face of his daughter, for whom Marie might be the only salvation.

Van Vliet was tempted to walk over, run over, to his daughter's aid. But it would only have made everything more chaotic, so he went on staring into the darkness and tried to hear what Marie was saying. She *must* have been saying something, after three years of complete silence she couldn't simply walk without a word past Lea into the house and close the door behind her. Or could she?

Marie was at the door, she seemed to be putting the key in the lock. Lea had stepped aside, she had had to press up against a bush and hold Nikki by the collar to let Marie past. It had stung her father when he saw her retreating like a slave who had no right to be there. Now he heard her saying something to Marie. In the half-open door, behind which the light had been turned on, Marie turned around and looked at Lea. A car drove past. ' . . . late . . . sorry . . . ' was all he could hear. Lea let go of the dog, stumbled over the leash, spread her arms out, it must have torn her father apart when he saw the pleading, yearning movement of his daughter, who didn't know what to do with herself and was making a foolish attempt simply to step outside of time and everything she did with people, and go on living where it hurt least.

Marie, a silhouette against the light coming from the door, seemed to straighten and become quite tall. Van Vliet had come to know and fear that straightening movement. 'No,' she said, and again: 'No.' Then she turned around, walked through the door and let it fall shut behind her.

For a long time Lea simply stood there, gazing at the door behind which the light went out. The fact that it went out – her father felt as if at that moment his daughter's every hope and future were destroyed. Now the light went on in the music room and Marie's outline became visible. Van Vliet recalled how a long time, a very long time ago, he had watched the shadow play that Marie and Lea performed in that room, and how he had felt excluded and envied them both the intimacy that spoke from their gestures. Now Lea, too, was standing outside, excluded by a light going out, a rejected little girl who could stagger and fall at any moment, both inside and out.

She set off in the wrong direction. It couldn't possibly get her home, neither could it take her to another comprehensible destination. Again Van Vliet's stomach tightened. The picture of his real daughter was overlaid with an imagined picture in which she walked further and further along that road, further and further, the street was an endless straight line, Lea walked and walked, the dog had disappeared, now his daughter's form slowly bleached away, became paler and paler, transparent, ethereal like the figure of a fairy, and then she was gone.

When he was finally able to shake off the picture, which had become more and more powerful, he felt as if he were waking up after a brief but intense illness.

'Later, when I lay awake,' he said, 'I thought about how my own mind was beginning to distort. It was very strange: I had expected panic at the thought – the fear of going insane. Instead I felt good about it. It wasn't exactly a feeling of happiness, more a kind of contentment, and I think it was the feeling that I was becoming similar to Lea – as preposterous as that might sound. Or perhaps I shouldn't say becoming similar, but rather *corresponding to*. Yes, that was it. It was the feeling of responding to my idea of Lea's infinite, fading path towards unreality that was spreading inexorably within my daughter. It was dangerous, I sensed that clearly. But that happens: that one willingly, devotedly and somehow contentedly faces the abyss.'

And then he talked about *Thelma and Louise*, the film in which two women, pursued by the police, hurtle towards the end of a canyon. They have communicated with few words, glances of complicity, they take each other by the hand and drive in inner harmony into deadly freedom.

'The image of those two hands,' he said, 'is one of the finest cinematic images that I know. It looks so easy and graceful, the way those two hands touch, it doesn't look at all like despair, more like happiness, a happiness that one can only acquire once one stakes everything, including one's life. A tremendous, foolhardy gambit with which the two women rise above all the power in the world, albeit only for the last seconds of their lives.'

Yes, Martijn, that is an image that must have touched your very depths. I see your hands in front of me, gripping the wheel when the lorries came, big, noisy and crushing.

Then Van Vliet had hailed a taxi, got the driver to drive it around the block and stop beside Lea. 'Oh, Dad,' was all she said, and got into the back seat with Nikki. She wasn't even slightly suspicious and apparently thought it was a chance meeting. They drove home in silence. He cooked, but she sat over her food with a glassy expression and left it at the end.

When he woke up towards morning, he heard a sound in the hall. In a corner, Lea was sitting on the floor beside Nikki, her arms wrapped around the dog, weeping. He carried her to bed and waited in the armchair until she had gone to sleep. It had been impossible to talk to her. 'She was unreachable now, unreachable by anyone,' he said.

22

IT WAS DURING those morning hours that the fatal thought came to him: he would buy Lea a violin made by Guarneri del Gesù – whatever the price.

The instrument – he must have thought – would restore his daughter and give her back the proud form and constitution that made up her true being. It would re-anchor her drifting, unmoored will. She would be back up at the top, building her incomparable cathedrals out of sacred notes. LEA VAN VLIET – he must have seen the proud, bright letters in front of him. David Lévy wouldn't be in the audience, and neither would Marie Pasteur, but he, her father, would. He still had no clear plan about how he might get hold of the money to buy one of the most expensive violins in the world. But he would do it. With a daring chess move he would keep his daughter from sliding into the darkness and bring her back to the world of the healthy.

There are ruses you can concoct, explanations you can recite to yourself in advance: the book about the Cremona violin-makers that he and Lea had read together at the kitchen table; Guarneri as a substitute for Armati; trumping Lévy; the ambition to see her on stage again; the desire to see her eyes gleaming again; the inexorable, even heinous will to eliminate all competitors and from now on to have her all to himself.

All these things ran through my mind. And yet: to be able to understand, really *understand* what Van Vliet did after that, you would have to have seen, heard and – however peculiar it sounds – smelled him. One might also say: you would have to have *sensed* him. You need to have seen him, the big, heavy man, defiantly clutching his hip flask, a gambler on the outside, and even more on the inside. You would have to have heard the vibration in his voice when he spoke the beloved, the sanctified name LEA, and the quite different vibration when he talked about Marie and Lévy. You would have to have seen his big hands on the bed covers and smelled his breath, sour with alcohol, which filled the nocturnal room, into which the protecting light fell from the bathroom. *What, damn it, do we know?* – you would also have to have heard the sound of those words, which come up more often in my memory than they do in reality. You would have to have experienced all that, in view of what happened next, to have the impression, the compelling impression that yes, this was precisely the thing that he had to do now.

I close my eyes, I summon him up in my mind and I think: yes, Martijn, that was how you *had* to feel and act, exactly like that. Because that is the rhythm of your soul. There were many other violins – they, too, noble instruments, which would have sounded good in Lea's hands, and they wouldn't have forced you to play that reckless, nonsensical game of poker. But no, it had to be a GUARNERI DEL GESÙ, because that was the name that had caught Lea's imagination at the kitchen table and distracted her attention from Amati and Lévy. Whatever the cost, it had to be a violin like Paganini's, the one displayed in Genoa City Hall. And I'm not surprised that the first thing you imagined, in the light of dawn beside Lea's bed, was how you would steal that violin from the display case. A Guarneri del Gesù. I've been with you for less than three days and it doesn't surprise me in the slightest that you saw this as your only option.

23

In the pale morning light Van Vliet sat down at his computer. The first few steps were child's play. A few clicks and the search engine brought him to the pages with the information he was looking for. There were 164 registered violins by Guarneri del Gesù. Only one was for sale, the dealer was in Chicago. To find out the price he had to join the website that collected all the information about old musical instruments. He hesitated. If he entered the number of his credit card, that would be a few dollars, not more. In spite of that, when he did it at last, he had the feeling that he was setting in motion things that would soon be out of his control.

The violin was valued at $1.8 million. Van Vliet sent an email to the dealer and asked what would happen if he wanted to buy the instrument. But it was the middle of the night in Chicago and he couldn't expect an answer before late afternoon.

When Lea woke up at about midday, it was as if nothing had happened. She seemed not to remember either the visit to Marie or the night-time scene with the dog. Van Vliet was startled. Never before had it been so clear to him that Lea's mind was falling to pieces, in sequences between which there was no connection. At the same time he was also relieved and delighted when he heard her on the phone, arranging to meet Caroline.

In the office he went through the documents about the millions he had raised. He was startled when he realized: even though he was unaware of it himself, from the very start he had been thinking about paying for the violin from his research money. He studied the sums on the screen: he would have to divert more than half the first tranche for the violin. That would mean delaying some of the projects and paying for them out of the second tranche. He stepped to the window and thought. When a colleague came in and glanced at the screen, Van Vliet flinched, even though there had been nothing suspicious on view. When he was alone again, he locked the whole folder with a password. Then he drove to a small private bank in Thun which he knew by name and opened a numbered account.

'When I stepped back into the street I had a feeling like the one I had when I sold shares to buy Lea's first full-size violin,' he said. 'Except that the feeling was much stronger, even though I hadn't done anything wrong, and everything could be revoked with a stroke of the pen.'

When he got back to the institute, Ruth Adamek complained that she no longer had access to the data because of the password. He coolly said something about security and shook his head when she asked him to tell him what it was. Afterwards he went over her words and glances in his mind. No, she couldn't possibly have been suspicious. She couldn't have known what he was thinking.

Towards evening the answer came from Chicago: the violin had been sold a few days before. On the way home Van Vliet felt disappointed and relieved in turn. He hid the bank documents from Thun in his bedroom. The danger seemed to have fled.

Caroline came round more often now, and Lea went off with her. Van Vliet became calmer. Perhaps he had read too much drama into Lea's visit to Marie. And wasn't it quite natural for her to seek consolation in her dog?

But then he met Caroline in town. She asked shyly whether they could go and have a coffee together. And then she talked about her fears for Lea. He gave a start, because he thought at first that she might have noticed something of the cracks and flaws in Lea's mind. But it wasn't that. It was Lea's memories of the concerts, the brilliance, the stage fright and the applause that worried Caroline. When they were together, it was all she talked about, for hours on end. She forgot everything that was going on around her and travelled back in time and blossomed as she did so; her eyes gleamed; she looked out of the café window into an imaginary future and drew up concert programmes, one after the other. When the time came to pay, it all vanished, she barely seemed to know where she was, and suddenly she seemed to Caroline like an old woman whose whole life was behind her. 'Caro,' she had said the last time they had parted, 'you'll help me, won't you?'

Van Vliet and Caroline were standing in the street. She saw what he was wondering. 'She thinks you're pleased. That the concerts are all done with, I mean. That you never liked all that. Because of David, David Lévy.'

Van Vliet spent the whole night in the institute. For the first few hours he battled with his rage against Lea. That you're pleased. How could she think something like that? Was it because he had missed a lot of concerts so that he wouldn't have to look at Lévy's salt-and-pepper mane? He paced up and down in his office, gazed out over the night-time city and talked to Lea. He talked and debated with her until his rage had subsided and he was left only with the horrible feeling that he had become quite a stranger to her. Her father, who had stood beside her in the station when Loyola de Colón had freed her from her torpor. Her father, whom she had asked at the kitchen table: 'Is a violin expensive?'

I think it was this feeling more than anything, this unbearable feeling of strangeness between them, that made Van Vliet set off again in the early hours of the morning in search of a violin that would bring his daughter back to life and prove to her that she had been mistaken, that she had misunderstood him. That violin was supposed to be the living, material proof that he really was willing to do *everything* to give her back her joy in music, her concert fever. And when he told me about the foolhardy, feverish resolution with which he sat down at the computer, for the first time I understood the weight of his hatred, which had flared up when the Maghrebi had said that sentence to him in his piercing voice: *C'est de votre fille qu'il s'agit.*

He found out that there was an internet forum for people who wanted to swap information and questions about the violins of the Guarneri family. With his eyes burning, he read the entire exchange.

'It was as if I were plunging into a hot, seething witch's cauldron,' he said. 'At the same time the language in the messages was cool and detached. There were rare, refined words in it. The whole thing reminded me of a secret lodge whose members followed special rules in their choice of words, which revealed them as initiates.'

And it was here that he encountered Signor Buio. 'Have you heard that Sig. Buio wants to sell his Guarneris at auction?' it said. 'Incredible, after all those years. There must be at least a dozen of them. All *Del Gesùs*. It's going to take place at his house, I've heard, and he only accepts cash. The whole thing seems to me as if he's planning a game of chess against the rest of the world, perhaps the last game of his life.'

Van Vliet hesitated before joining in, because then they would have his address. But it was just too strong.

What he discovered was a story from a book of fairy tales. Signor Buio was a legendary man from Cremona who had been given that name – Mr Dark – because he never appeared wearing anything other than black: shabby black suit, worn black shoes that looked like slippers, black shirt and above it the wise, wrinkled neck of a man who must have between eighty and ninety. As rich as Croesus and as tight as a miser. A flat in a shabby house with damp walls. He's said to keep the violins in cupboards and under the bed. One *filius Andreae* was supposed to have been crushed by the bedsprings.

He trudged through Cremona with a plastic bag with holes in it, in which he brought home cheap vegetables, scraps of meat and a bottle of rotgut. No sign of a wife, but according to rumours a daughter whom he idolized, even though she denied his existence. He carried the banknotes, folded several times, in a tiny red wallet. There were a thousand hypotheses about why it was red and not black. When a waiter refused to take one of these crumpled banknotes, Signor Buio bought the café and threw him out.

He claimed to be related to Caterina Rota, the wife of Guarneri del Gesù. And he hated all foreign companies that dealt in violins from Cremona. When he discovered that a dealer owned a Guarneri, his hatred was boundless and he dreamed of hiring someone to steal it and bring it home. No one knew why, but he nurtured a particular hatred of American dealers in Chicago, Boston and New York. He couldn't speak English, but he knew all the swear words. According to legend there had been an Italian woman violinist whose playing he loved above all and with whom he had become besotted. He recognized every Cremona violin by its tone and could hear whose hands had produced it. So he knew that she was playing on a Guarneri *filius Andreae*. Hardly a day passed when he didn't put on a record by her. One day he learned that she had bought the violin from a dealer in Boston. He shattered all her records with an axe and tore her photographs into a thousand pieces. Everyone said: he's gone mad, but there's no one on the planet who knows more about Cremona violins.

Van Vliet enquired about the date and location of the auction. It was to be held in three days, and begin at midnight. The house had no number, but was recognizable by its blue front door. That Sig. Buio only accepted cash: did that mean that people came here with briefcases full of money? No one really knew, but it must have been so.

Van Vliet felt as if he had taken a drug that both pepped him up and made him incredibly tired. He closed the office door and lay down on the sofa. The scraps of dreams were vague and faded quickly, but in the end they were always about the dark man who wanted money that he didn't have on him. He didn't hear the old man's malicious giggles, but they were there.

He woke up when Ruth Adamek knocked on the door. She gave him a curious look when he opened the door with an exhausted face and ruffled hair. Again she asked about the password. Again he refused. Now they were not only adversaries, but inches away from being enemies. He deleted the password that she might perhaps have been able to guess and replaced it with a new one that she'd never happen upon: DELGESÙ. Then he drove home.

24

'IF LEA HADN'T BEEN SITTING on the bed with that face when I got home – perhaps I wouldn't have done it,' Van Vliet said.

We had booked our hotel rooms for one more night and were sitting in mine. The closer his story got to catastrophe, the more often he paused. We had sometimes walked by the lake for half an hour, without a word from him. Now and again he had taken a swig from his hip flask, but only a swig. It was impossible to drive to Bern now. He would have frozen and his story would have dried up. So I led him back to the hotel. When I gave him his key, he threw me a timid and grateful glance.

'She was sitting there with her legs drawn up, surrounded by photographs of her performances,' he now continued.

'Some pictures of her playing, others of her taking a bow, still others in which the conductor was kissing her hand. There were so many of them and they were so densely packed together that they looked like a second blanket in which there was only a gap for a cowering body, a small gap, because she had almost stopped eating by then and was getting thinner and thinner. Her expression was empty and remote, making me think: *She's been sitting like that for hours.*

'She gave me a look that immediately reminded me of Caroline's words: *that you're pleased.* If only it had been a furious look! A look that could have sparked a struggle, like the ones I had had with her in the office at night. But it was a look almost entirely without reproach, only full of disappointment, a look without a future. I asked if she wanted me to cook something. She shook her head almost unnoticeably, it was little more than an echo of a shake of the head. Then, when I was standing in the kitchen, pursued by her gaze, I thought something I had never thought before, and it hurt so much that I had to get a hold of myself. What I was thinking was: *She wanted a different father.* Do you understand now that I had to get to Cremona? That I simply HAD TO?'

I hadn't given him a sign that I didn't understand, quite the contrary. But the closer we came to the deed with which he had crossed a boundary, the more I became for him, it seemed to me, a judge, in the end a judge whose understanding could be wooed and whom one could finally win over. He sat on the edge of my bed, his hands clutching the hip flask between his knees. He barely looked at me, talking to the carpet. But every movement I made in the armchair irritated him, his concentration flickered, a hint of annoyance darted across his weary features.

Back then, he had slowly closed the door to the flat behind him and gone back to the institute. He locked himself in the office and with a click of the mouse transferred half of the research money to his account in Thun. 'That one tap of the finger on the mouse key,' he said hoarsely, 'one tap among hundreds of thousands, indistinguishable from all the others and yet elevated from them – I will never forget it. My facial muscles as I tapped will stay in my memory for ever. They tensed. They felt hot.'

Martijn van Vliet, who had lain on the bed as a boy and dreamed of being a forger. Martijn van Vliet, who took on all challengers in chess and could not resist the temptation to play a foolhardy gambit incomprehensible to his opponent. Now, immediately after that fateful click of the mouse, he was frightened. It must have been an infernal fear. It was still visible as a shadow in his dark gaze.

But he drove. First to Thun and then, with a briefcase full of banknotes, to Cremona.

I looked at him as he sat on the edge of the bed and told me about the Italian customs man who walked past the compartment without deigning to glance at him. Beneath a clear, blue sky he had driven through the Po Valley, dizzy with excitement. There was fear in it, too, the fear of the mouse click, but the further south he went, the more it gave way to the fever of the gambler.

'I smoked. I held my head into the wind. I smoked and drank from the cardboard cup the lousy coffee from the drinks car.' His hands clenched around the hip flask, his knuckles were white.

It was strange: there was the strength, indeed the violence of his big hands, which expressed both the guilty conscience and his fury over the guilty conscience. It was there, between his knees, that the battle with the inner judge was raging. And above it, at the level of gaze and voice, all the words now came, words in which one could feel the airstream of a journey that had driven him into the craziest adventure of his whole life. I looked away from those white knuckles. I didn't want him to lacerate himself. I wanted him to live, to live. I thought of Liliane and other opportunities when I had not lived as I might have lived and perhaps should have lived.

'It was insane, completely crazy, to go at midnight with a briefcase full of embezzled money to an auction held by a twisted, morbidly avaricious old man, to bid for one of the most expensive violins in the world. In fact, my going there couldn't possibly be true. But it was true. I heard my footsteps on the cobbles, and when I listened to their quiet echo in the deserted alley, I saw ahead of me the street that Lea had walked along when she was coming from Marie's and turned in the wrong direction. Now, once more, the endless, straight street faded away, the glow of that distant, fading image settled over the dull glimmer of the bare bulbs that meagrely illuminated the alley in Cremona in place of street lamps. And now, too, I felt once more how perfectly the unreality of my nocturnal walk matched the unreality that was spreading within Lea.'

Van Vliet closed his eyes. Noisy guests walked past the door. He waited until it was quiet again.

'I wish I hadn't done it. It destroyed so much. It destroyed everything. And yet: I wouldn't like to miss the moment when I walked through the blue door, climbed the stairs between damp walls and knocked on the old man's door. It was as if I were experiencing a completely lucid dream in a state of extreme alertness, and standing weightless, supported only by absurdity, in an imaginary room, which could have been a room in a painting by Chagall, a fairy-tale room, terribly beautiful. And I wouldn't like to miss the hours that followed either; those crazy, nonsensical hours when I threw all the others out of the running.'

The old man lived in two rooms, separated by a sliding door. The door was open so that the seven men bidding had room on their rickety chairs. It was still so cramped that they inevitably came into contact with one another. It must have been stuffy, there were dust devils all over the place, and the sour smell of old man came from every corner. One of the men, whose nausea was plain to see, got up without a word and left.

Signor Buio, dressed exactly as legend said, sat in a greasy-looking reclining chair in the corner. From there he had a view of everything, and could turn the gaze from his bright eyes – which seemed to bleach still further as the night wore on, assuming an increasingly crazy appearance – upon each individual. No one had been greeted as they entered; the door had been opened as if by some ghostly hand, by an inconspicuous girl who stood there as if there were no one else in the room. No one seemed to know anyone else, no one introduced themselves, they gave each other alienated, calculating and suspicious looks.

Van Vliet related it in such a way that I thought: *He enjoyed this surreal situation.*

'It was a bit like a gathering of bats. We didn't really see each other, we just heard and sensed one another,' he said. It was, I think, that absolute, ghostly strangeness that he enjoyed. Not the way one enjoys something pleasant. It was more like pouncing on something and clinging to it, even if it turns out that a raven-black, desperate conjecture corresponded to the truth.

In his case it was the conjecture of a final, unbridgeable strangeness between people. And, in fact, it is wrong to call it a conjecture. In him it was more like a seasoned experience, the dregs of all other feelings. I never heard the word *strangeness* pass his lips. But if I close my eyes and listen to his story as if listening to a piece of music, it becomes clear to me that he was speaking about nothing but that strangeness. He had known it as a ragamuffin and a latchkey child. Then came the teacher who gave him the books about Louis Pasteur and Marie Curie. After that it was Jean-Louis Trintignant and Cécile. And above all, for a few years, there was Lea, whom he experienced – or wanted to experience – as a bulwark against strangeness, until she said *à très bientôt* to Lévy in the rose garden, and he had to hear her vulgar outbursts, before learning at last from Caroline that she misunderstood him in such an incomprehensible manner. And then that same man, with millions in stolen notes, set off on a journey in order to possess, with that Guarneri del Gesù, that object – a truly magical object – that was the only thing that could sweep away that misunderstanding and overcome the strangeness, and landed in a gathering of bats which showed him the apogee of strangeness in a raw and unmistakeable form. *That* – this fulminating, outrageous paradox – was what he was enjoying. It must have been a dizzying experience, a vertigo of loneliness, a rushing downward spiral of self-lacerating insight. And yes: Martijn van Vliet was the very man to enjoy such a thing.

I asked him what it would be like if a feeling of strangeness opened up between him and me. And it would open up. I closed my eyes, listened and imagined we were driving through the Camargue, rice fields and water on either side, with the drifting clouds reflected in them beneath a tall sky. *Le bout du monde*. We should have stayed down there, laughing by the white wall and drinking with the light behind us, and the ending would have been like the frozen image at the end of a film.

'The violins came out of a big ship's chest that stood beside the old man's chair,' Van Vliet went on. 'Anchors painted on the sides, flaking paint. A huge thing, certainly a metre high and at least twice as long. Inside that chest – and not in the cupboard or under the bed, as people said – lay the violins, and they were carefully layered, with soft cloths in between.

The enormous brass clasps squeaked as the old man opened the box and took out the first violin.

'It was a violin by Pietro Guarneri, Andrea's oldest son and the uncle of del Gesù. I remembered, because he was the one I knew least about and the one least written about in the book I brought home from Milan.

'"*Mille milioni!*" cried the old man, this was back in the days of the lira. The price was right for one of the less valuable Guarneris. But the longer the night drew on, the more clearly I understood that those words meant much more to the old man than the mere statement of a price. They were words which, of course, meant a great deal of money, but beyond that they stood for a round, glowing unit of wealth, the primal unit of wealth, the idea of money per se. *Mille milioni* – that was the ultimate sum of money, behind which there could be no larger one. *Due mila milioni, tre mila milioni* – that would, even though it was a multiple, be less.

'The violin was bought by a man in a suit that must have been Armani and which was completely out of place in this shabby setting. Apart from me and a Frenchman, the men were all Italians, judging by their language at least. But then one of them, rummaging through his papers for something, dropped his passport on the floor, not far from the old man's feet. It was an American passport. "*Fuori!*" he shouted. "*Fuori!*" The man wanted to explain, defend himself, but the old man repeated his cry, and at last the man left. The atmosphere in the room was icy, even though we were sweating.

'The inconspicuous girl, who had entered silently and sat down at the table in the corner, wrote everything down. The violins passed from hand to hand, the others all had little torches in the form of fountain pens, which they shone inside the violin to see the label. These men were experienced. They weren't about to be bamboozled. You could tell by the way their hands ran along the *c*-bouts and the *f*-holes, felt their way along the scrolls and tested the lacquer. And yet the room was filled with suspicion. Most of the men, before they bid, leaned back and studied the old man through half-closed eyes and with expressions of disdain. What was the situation regarding certificates of authenticity? one of them wanted to know. "*Sono io il certificato*," I'm the certificate, the old man said. In fact, he never bought without first hearing a violin, said an elderly, elegant-looking man whom one could easily have imagined in a Venetian palazzo. No one was forced to buy, the old man replied dryly, in a tone of great finality.

'The Guarneri del Gesù was the ninth or tenth to come out of the box. I borrowed a torch. JOSEPH GUARNERIUS FECIT CREMONAE ANNO 1743 †HIS, it said on the yellowing label. It must have been one of his last works, he had died in 1744, not far from here. Could one forge such a label and somehow work it into the violin retrospectively? It was a smaller format; the measuring tape did the rounds. Shallow top and bottom arching, open *c*-bouts, short corners, long *f*-holes, magnificent lacquer. The typical features. There was also a lighter patch where the chin-rest had been, as in *Il Cannone*, which Paganini had played.

'"*Mille milioni e mille milioni e mille milioni!*" the old man croaked. How he loved and enjoyed those words! I was starting to like him. I was still suspicious, however. The croaking, I was sure of it by now, was show, a show for us poor lunatics who came dancing to him in the middle of the night to satisfy our greed for Guarneris. What else was show?

'Three billion lire. That was almost as much as I had on me. The most expensive Del Gesù had brought in £6 million at Sotheby's in London. Compared to that, this was a bargain. I wanted to have it. I thought of how I had sat with Lea at the kitchen table, studying *Il Cannone*. At first she had been bothered by the lighter patch, then she had said: "In fact, it's quite good. It's somehow authentic and alive, you can almost feel the warmth of Niccolò's chin." I wanted to sit with her at the kitchen table again. She had to close her eyes; I laid this violin on the table in front of her, then she was allowed to open her eyes. She got to her feet and our flat turned into a cathedral of sacred Guarneri notes. All the dullness, all the emptiness, had fled from her gleaming eyes; the bad things of recent times were forgotten; Lévy was the distant past; it was as if Marie's "*No!*" had never happened; the photographed scenes on the bed had faded to shadows. *I had to have that violin*. From now on there would be nothing but the open, happy future of LEA VAN VLIET, which was much more radiant than the past of Mademoiselle Bach. And this new Lea van Vliet would return to the scene with a violin that far surpassed her old Amati. *I had to have it, whatever the cost.*'

He darted me a timid, questioning look: did I understand? I nodded. *Of course* I understood, Martijn. No one who heard you speaking of it could have failed to understand. Now that I am writing it down, the tears that I held back for so long are coming at last. You were sitting once again behind the wheel of the racing car that Jean-Louis Trintignant drove from the Côte d'Azur to Paris, a man who *had given everything, simply everything*, as you said, and once again you searched the whole city to find the Dior perfume that Cécile had used.

Why didn't you call me?

'I started bidding. It was the first time, so far I had only sat silently among the others, in retrospect it seems to me as if I were floating on my uncomfortable chair in an imaginary room, in a room from a Chagall painting, somewhere at mid-height, held up by nothing but the absurdity of the situation. And now I entered the real, hot room, in which you could have cut the air with a knife and the smell was enough to make you throw up.

'I had held the violin in my hands until the others had become uneasy. When my eyes now met the old man's, I thought: *He has noticed how much it means to me.* Was that a smile that spoke from those bright eyes, from that cadaverous face? I didn't know, but the expression made me go on bidding, more and more, the sum was now far greater than the amount in my briefcase, but the old man's face gave me the desperate courage to keep going. *He will defer the balance*, I thought vaguely, as I crossed the five billion threshold. Five billion lire, about four million francs – any sum was possible now. I had arrived in a different imaginary room, the room of feather-light play money, which is worth everything and nothing. The horrendous sum was reflected in the worried faces of the others. But I became more and more relaxed. It was a hurtling roller-coaster ride. I leaned back and enjoyed the prospect of soon being carried out of the curve and far beyond to where things faded away. In the end I was the only one still bidding. Six billion lire, a good four and a half million francs. The girl looked around, then wrote down the sum.

'The old man looked at me. His gaze was not as piercing as it had been earlier in the night. There was no smile in his eyes either. But there was something gentle in his eyes, a benevolence that was difficult to interpret, and above it his bright eyes suddenly looked into the world quite normally. The madness in his gaze had gone, making me think: *That glint of insanity is, like the croaking, mere show. The old man may be twisted, the box of violins proves as much, but he isn't crazy and he's playing us all for fools.*

'"*I violini non sono in vendita,*" the violins are not for sale. The old man said it quietly and yet very clearly. After that he pursed his lips into a mocking, contemptuous grin. I don't know why it didn't come as a complete surprise to me. The old man seemed to me to be more and more like a gambler, a clown, a charlatan. But the others sat there as if they'd been slapped. No one said a word. I looked over at the girl: was she in on it, was she there to give the show the appearance of authenticity?

'The man in the Armani suit was the first to spring to life. He was white with rage. "*Che impertinenza . . .* " he murmured, knocking over his chair as he rose to his feet and stormed out. Two others got up, stood there for a while and looked at the old man as if they wanted to wring his neck. The gentleman I had imagined in the Venetian palazzo had stayed in his seat and was struggling with his feelings. Judging by his appearance there must have been fury inside him, but there was also an attempt to see the matter humorously. In the end he, too. left, the only one who could bring himself to say *Buona notte!*

'I had stayed on my chair, I don't know why. Perhaps because of the way the old man had looked at me at the end. He acted as if I weren't there any more either, rose to his feet with surprisingly elastic movements and opened the windows. Cool night air streamed in; the first ray of sunlight was visible above the rooftops. I didn't know what to say or do. I didn't actually know what it was that I wanted. I had just made up my mind to go when the old man stepped in front of me and offered me a cigarette. "*Fumi?*" Not a trace of a croak now, and the familiar form of address sounded like a vague promise.

'He was just an old miser who enjoyed being a miser with a heap of money. I had the impression that this was the only thing he had been able to enjoy in his life. Not that he said anything about himself. And asking him questions – that was forbidden by the field of tension that surrounded him and which, if he were handled badly, could make him dangerous. Instead he asked me why I wanted to have the Del Gesù at any price.

'What was I supposed to do? Either I told him about Lea or I left. And so, in the early hours of the morning, in which

I heard the steeple clock chiming, I told a twisted, stinking rich old Italian man, sitting in a shabby hole in Cremona with a case full of violins beside him, the story of my daughter's entire misfortune.'

Back then, in the hotel room, I didn't notice, but I feel it now: I was jealous of the old man and disappointed that I wasn't the only one Van Vliet had told about the terrible things that had happened to his daughter. I was glad that Signor Buio could not have heard what was still to come.

'The old man pointed to the table where the girl had been writing. Only now did I see that it was also a chess table. "Do you play?" I nodded. "Let's make a deal," he said. "One game, only one. You win – you get the Del Gesù for nothing; you lose – you pay me *mille milioni* for it." He got some pieces and set them up.

'It would be the most important game of my life.

'I don't want to describe how I felt. I could pay back all the money in Thun and transfer it over and delete the password. It would be as if it had never happened. And still Lea would open her eyes at the kitchen table, pick up the violin and turn the flat into a Guarneri cathedral. It was insane. My God, it was so insane that I had to go to the toilet every few minutes, even though nothing more was coming. The old man, on the other hand, just sat almost motionless by the board with his eyes half-closed.

'He opened with the Sicilian Defence. We played nine or ten moves, then he was exhausted and had to go to bed, so we arranged to meet in the evening. Thus began three completely mad days. Days of chess trance, of euphoria and anxiety, days lived entirely for the next evening, when the game continued. I bought a board and pieces, moved to a quieter hotel, bought myself a chess manual and went through all the things that could help me to win this mad game, which the old man was playing with great finesse and control as if it were nothing at all. After the second night I took a sleeping pill and slept for twelve hours, then it started all over again.

'I went to the cathedral, suddenly hungry for devotional music. I saw Marie drawing the cross on Lea's forehead. When I closed my eyes and sensed the huge space with its bracing chill and the smell of incense, I felt as if I were sitting in the middle of the cathedral that Lea always built with her clear, warm notes the moment she put bow to string – a cathedral that offered her protection against life, and which at the same time was life.

'There was a record on sale, in which the music of Bach was played on famous Cremona violins, so that one could compare. I lay on the bed and heard the different sounds: Guarneri, Amati, Stradivarius. It takes time to be able to distinguish them. Of course, I knew that not all Guarneris sound the same, and neither do all Del Gesùs. Still, with the Guarneri sound on the record, I travelled back to our kitchen and let Lea build her cathedral. The notes were sepia, that struck me as obvious, even if I couldn't have explained it to anyone.

'It was at the end of the second note that I felt: *I'm going to lose*. Although when I left the game, it didn't look entirely certain. But there was something compelling about the old man's features, which I just resisted, without being able to break the style of his attack. I analysed the game in my hotel room for hours, and later, too, I played through it again dozens of times. I could repeat it to you like a child's rhyme, kept not only in one's head, but in one's whole body. I made no obvious errors, but neither did I come up with the big idea that could have turned the whole thing around. We were playing with jade figures, the only luxury to be seen anywhere around. And there was something unsettling about them: in them, ordinary green jade was mixed with rare reddish jade, reddish veins ran through the green bodies of the pieces. It was disturbing to the eyes and somehow also to the thoughts, and all the time I had the feeling that I lacked that last bit of concentration I could normally muster over a chessboard. But in fact it can't have been that, because even over the board at the hotel I couldn't find the solution. Eventually, I ran out of Parisiennes, and all the other cigarettes I tried threw me into a state of confusion. And even at home, with a Parisienne between my lips, it got no better. He was just too good for me.

'At about four o'clock on the last night I looked at him. He read capitulation in my eyes. "*Ecco!*" he said and smiled languidly. He too was exhausted. He fetched two glasses and filled them with grappa. Our eyes met.

'When I think that during those minutes I might have been able to change his mind and persuade him to give me the violin! Spending three nights facing someone over a chess-board, the eternities of waiting for the next move, attempting to penetrate the other person's thoughts, his plans and feints, his thoughts about his own thoughts, the other as a target for one's own hope and anxiety – it had all created a great sense of intimacy, from which it might perhaps have been possible. A different word from me, a different stress and everything could have been different. Something in my story about Lea had touched the old man. When I think of him it's as a man in which there were many seasoned emotions, a lot of sediment, thick layers of it, and some of that had been swirled up, perhaps because of the daughter he worshipped – who, rumour said, existed – or perhaps for no reason. Perhaps I could have persuaded him to give the violin not to me, but to Lea, so to speak. He had sat there in silence when I told him of the evening when she came back from Neuchâtel without the Amati.

'But I messed it up, damn it. I messed it up. *You need to open up more, Martijn,* Cécile often said. *You can't expect people to go running after you to guess your feelings. You need to open up more to me, too, otherwise things will go wrong between us,* she said. Particularly towards the end. When I walked down the long hospital corridor to her room on my last visit, I firmly resolved to tell her how much she meant to me. But then those words came: "You must promise me that you will look after . . . " Then I couldn't go on, I just couldn't do it. *Merde.* And where would I have learned it from? My mother was from the Ticino. There were outbursts of rage, but the language of emotions, the ability to say how one was feeling – no one showed me that.'

He gave me a quizzical look. 'Me neither,' I said. And then I asked him why he didn't tell the old man about the fraud. He might have been impressed.

'Yes, I wondered that too, on the way back. In fact, he was exactly the right man for that. It must have been because the whole business weighed so heavily on me and pursued me into my sleep. Again and again in my dreams Ruth Adamek asked me for the password and it was clearly legible on her face: she knew *everything*. That was why. I considered taking the train back to Milan and going to talk to him again. But asking him to give me back the money – no, that was out of the question. The fact that he now had the money made it impossible.'

Van Vliet took a bite from the meal that we had ordered from room service. It was clear: he was oscillating between hunger and revulsion.

'Someone should write down the whole business about money. Just tell the whole story: poverty, wealth, the euphoria of gold, loss, fraud, shame, humiliation, unwritten rules – everything. In a straight line. Unadorned. The whole damned story about the poison of money. How it gnaws away at the emotions.'

He had counted out the money for Signor Buio on the table – *mille milioni* – a good deal, soberly viewed. A pile of banknotes lying there on the table. The old man hadn't greedily grabbed for it; he had left the money where it was and considered it in a posture that clearly said he didn't care whether he had it or not, he didn't need it.

'That was the very last moment,' Van Vliet said, 'and I let it go by.'

When changing trains in Milan he was haunted by the thought that someone might bump into the violin and break it. He anxiously put the case under his arm and pressed it to him. It was a shabby case, a match for the old man. He had seen Van Vliet thinking that it was shabby. '*Il suono!*' he said mockingly. The sound is what matters.

The other people in the train didn't pay any particular attention to the violin or the briefcase. None the less, his shirt was drenched in sweat when he got out of the train in Thun. He paid in the remaining money, then drove to Bern and went straight to Krompholz to have the violin restrung.

Katharina Walther looked in perplexity at the shabby case, then opened it.

'I don't think she knew straight away that she had a Guarneri in front of her. But she could tell that it was a valuable instrument. She looked at me and said nothing. Then she went to the back of the shop. When she came back, there was a strange expression on her face. "A Del Gesù," she said, "a real *Guarneri del Gesù*." Her eyes narrowed slightly. "It must have cost a fortune."

'I nodded and looked at the floor. She wasn't Ruth Adamek in the dream, she couldn't have known. In that night's dream, of course, she knew. And that was why there was something judgemental and menacing in her words when she said, "You shouldn't do that, not under any circumstances." In fact, she said something different: "To make her forget the Amati,

I see that. Still . . . I don't know . . . don't you think it might be . . . let's say . . . too taxing for her? That it will make her think she has to get back into that crazy orbit? I don't want to get involved, but don't you think she should find herself first? How long is it since you bought the little one her first violin? Twelve, thirteen years? All a bit breathless, I always thought, and then you told me about that crisis . . . But of course, we'll have the violin restrung for you by this evening, it will be an honour for my colleague, he's over the moon."

'Why didn't I listen to her?'

Van Vliet drove to the office and transferred the rest of the money back into the research account. Ruth Adamek walked past him in the corridor without a word. He lay down on the sofa, waking up shortly afterwards with his heart thumping. For the first time he had the feeling that his heart might give up on him one day.

Katharina Walther brought him the violin in a new, elegant case. On the house, as she said. And she apologized for her intervention. Her colleague came over. He had been playing on it. 'That tone,' was all he said, 'that sound.'

Van Vliet drove home. Before he went upstairs, he sat down in the café on the corner. After two or three sips he left his coffee on the table. Then he went upstairs and into the flat with one of the most valuable violins in the world, which was supposed to put everything right again.

25

LEA HAD BEEN SLEEPING. She slept at the most impossible times, then wandered through the flat at night and startled the dog. Now she looked at her father in confusion, with a sleep-drunk, unsteady gaze. 'You were away so . . . I didn't know . . . ' she said thickly. Her father later found empty wine bottles in the kitchen.

'I thought back to those nights long ago when I sat at the computer until I heard her calm breathing,' Van Vliet said. 'Compared with today, what a happy time that was! More than ten years had passed since then. I stood there, I saw my sleepy and slightly unkempt daughter in front of me and wished more than anything that I could turn back time. For ages after that when I lay awake at night, I bargained with the devil to make that wish come true: to be able to travel back with Lea to before the day when we heard Loyola de Colón in the station. He could have had my soul in return. I imagined that journey in time so vividly that for a few moments I managed to believe it. Then, in my half-sleep, I experienced happy moments. I wanted to have more and more of those. So I became addicted to those day-dreaming travels through time.'

But the important thing now was to make the other day-dream come true: Lea taking the Guarneri, getting up and filling the flat with its sacred notes. She was awake now and glanced questioningly at the violin case. Van Vliet made coffee as she got dressed. When, as if instructed to do so, she sat down with her eyes closed at the kitchen table, he set down the violin in front of her, then sat facing her and gave the order.

For a long time she didn't say a word. She ran her fingers mutely over the contours of the instrument. When she stroked the pale patch of the chin-rest with her hand, Van Vliet hoped for a sign of recognition, a remark about *Il Cannone*. But Lea's face remained expressionless, her eyes dull. He walked behind her and shone a torch inside. She held the violin at an angle and read the label. Her breathing grew faster. She took the torch from his hand and directed the beam of light inside. The longer it went on, the more hope stirred in Van Vliet: the letters with the big, holy name would penetrate inside her and then she would explode with surprise and joy. But it went on and on and suddenly fear welled up in him, the same fear as before, when he had listened through the crack in the door and heard her calling Nikki Niccolò. Was she already too mired in herself to be gripped once more by the magic of that enchanted name?

In the end her silence must have become too much for Van Vliet; he went into the bedroom and closed the door. A crime and an insane journey, all for nothing. Weariness washed over him, numb disappointment and despair, and in the end he fell asleep.

When Lea started playing in the middle of the night, he was immediately wide awake and dashed into the hallway. She had pushed all the furniture in the music room up against the wall and was standing in one of her long, black concert dresses, with her hair done and make-up on her face. She was playing Bach's E major Partita. For a moment Van Vliet must have had a sense of doom, because that was the music that Loyola de Colón had played. It was, he thought, not good that the new start consisted of a memory, a return to the music that had first awakened her. There was something ritualistic about it, something impersonal; she was merely its vehicle, rather than being entirely herself in the choice of the new notes. But then he was overwhelmed by the warm, golden sounds that seemed to burst the walls with their power and clarity. And he was even more overwhelmed by the concentration on Lea's face. After months in which that face had lost all its tension and had prematurely aged, it was once again the face of Lea van Vliet, the radiant violinist who filled whole auditoria.

And yet there was also something that worried him when he sat down on a chair in the hall and watched her through the open door.

'Why had she needed to do herself up as if she were standing in the concert hall? She had cut her nails; it was a great relief to see that. It is terrible, a message of pure despair, when a violinist lets her nails grow until she can't play any more. But the dress, the face powder, the lipstick – and all of that in the middle of the night?

'For months she had lived cowering away, inwardly and often outwardly as well. Now she had pulled herself together and connected once more with the layer of herself that she had previously shown to the world. When I looked at her and listened to her back then, worried about the ghostly character of the nocturnal scene, that thought took shape in me: My daughter, she is a creature of layers; she consists of spiritual layers, she lives on various plateaux that she can enter and leave, and now she has found her way back to the plateaux that had long lain empty and unlit, a little like the platform of an abandoned railway station.

'I studied the play of expressions on her face, no longer as fluid as before, and which, with its occasional faltering pauses, bore within it the traces of her earlier torpor. And then for the first time I thought yet another thought, which I would think often over the next while and which would startle me afresh each time: She has no control over that switch of layers; she isn't the director of this drama; if she steps on to her inner plateau or if she leaves it, it's a pure happening, comparable to a geological shift for which no one is responsible.

'Perhaps you will think – and I myself sometimes thought it too: That's how it is for all of us. And that is also true. But in the internal drama that was now unfolding within Lea, there were breaks and abrupt, jerky changes that cast a particularly harsh light on the fact that the soul was far more of a place where things happened than one where things were done.'

Van Vliet was silent for a while, and then said something that has remained particularly clearly in my memory, because it expressed a fearlessness in his thinking that was part of his being: 'The experience of inner seamlessness – it is down to the mercurial fluidity of change and virtuosity with which we immediately retouch all the cracks until they can't be seen. And that virtuosity is all the greater in that it knows nothing of itself.'

I consider the picture of him leaning against the lamp, a drinking man against the light. The snot-nosed street urchin and the devious chess player had become someone who knew how fragile the life of the mind really is, and how many stop-gaps and deceptions we must go through before we somehow come to terms with ourselves. A man who, on the basis of this insight, felt great solidarity with everyone else – even though I never heard that word from him and he would have rejected it outright. Yes, I think he would have rejected it; it would have struck him as too fussy. None the less, it is the right word for the thing he felt growing inside him that night, and which from now on, beyond all affection and admiration, bound him with his daughter, who enchanted the whole house with her notes played on the Guarneri that night.

First of all the man who lived above them had furiously rung the doorbell. He had moved in only recently and knew nothing about Lea. Van Vliet did something disarming: he pulled him in and offered him a chair from which he could see Lea. He sat there in his pyjamas and grew quieter and quieter. Through the open door the music filled the whole staircase, and when Van Vliet looked out, the other tenants who knew about Lea were sitting on the steps, putting their fingers to their lips if anyone made an annoying noise. The applause filled the staircase. 'Encore!' someone called.

Van Vliet hesitated. Was it all right to disturb Lea in her imaginary concert hall? Was whatever had built up inside her not far too fragile? But Lea had heard the clapping and now stepped into the stairway with her rustling dress. She bowed, started playing, and didn't stop until another hour had passed. Meantime her facial expressions were as lively and fluid as before; one could see and hear her becoming more and more familiar with the instrument from one minute to the next. She chose pieces of a rising level of difficulty, the old virtuosity was back, and even though people were beginning to shiver, they sat where they were.

'It was the first concert after the breakdown,' Van Vliet said. 'In a way the most beautiful. My daughter was stepping out of the darkness and into the light.'

MADEMOISELLE BACH IS BACK! read the newspaper headlines. Agents scrambled for her. Lea could hardly move for offers. Was that what Van Vliet had wanted?

He had thought about that. Soon, however, he noticed that he had not won back his daughter as he had hoped. She was celebrating her moments of success, that wasn't the issue.

But she didn't seem to be quite herself. Porcelain – that was the world that he used over and over again when he talked about that time. She and her actions seemed to consist of translucent porcelain: filigree, precious and very fragile. He nurtured the hope that there might be a solid core behind it, which would remain if the porcelain shattered. But increasingly the hope made way for fear that there was nothing behind it but an opening void, a void into which his daughter was disappearing for ever.

Lea's skin, which had always been very white, became still paler, almost transparent, and at the temple, more and more often, a bluish vein appeared, throbbing, with strange irregularity, a rhapsodic twitch, the harbinger of an event in which all order would be lost. And even though her new notes were praised to the skies: there was something wrong with them, her father felt. At last he worked out what it was: 'Now that the music was no longer framed by the love of Marie and Lévy, now that it was no longer carried and supported by that love, to my ears it sounded impersonal, glassy and cold. Sometimes I thought: It sounds as if Lea were standing in front of a pale, dry wall of hard, cold slate. There was nothing even Joseph Guarneri could do about it. It wasn't to do with the violin. It was to do with her.'

There were exceptions. Evenings when everything sounded as it had done before, played from within. But then there was something else that troubled Van Vliet: it seemed to him as if, in her mind, Lea were playing Lévy's Amati – as if the Guarneri had become the crystallization point of the delusion that everything was fine with Lévy again. The new violin, which was supposed to have been a liberating counterweight to the past, had – he thought at such moments – become a new centre of gravity for the old fantasies.

Even though he had been given instructions to the contrary, her agent revealed to the press what kind of violin it was. Van Vliet's colleagues read it and in their eyes he could read the question of where he had got the money. Through the open door of Aaron's office he saw that she was studying the whole web page from which he had found his information about the violins made by the Guarneri family. During the night he changed the password for the file containing his research money. He turned DELGESÙ into ÙSEGLED and later ÙSEDGL.

He could feel it: it was a time bomb. He could cover up the gap in the finances for a few months, perhaps a year, not more than that. He thought of bills from a dummy corporation. He started playing the lottery. A kind of bank phobia settled in and became apparent in the fact that he had mental blocks about internet banking and made mistakes when performing the simplest of operations. The name THUN often flickered through his dreams.

If the worst came to the worst, he said to himself, he could still sell the violin. In fact, the idea of taking it away from Lea again was unthinkable, and when he thought of the words he would have to say, he grew dizzy. But it was worth millions and the thought of that managed to calm him down in spite of everything.

There were concerts abroad. Paris, Milan, Rome. The organizers and agents didn't like the fact that the father was there. Not that they said anything. But their handshakes were cool and reserved and they pointedly addressed only the daughter. It didn't let up: now Lea seemed grateful for his presence, now she made him feel she would rather have been travelling without him. There were happy moments when she laid her head upon his shoulder. There were humiliating moments when she just left him there, chatting to the conductor.

In Rome he would have liked to go with her to the church on the little piazza from which he had heard the music that had broken the ice and realigned his feelings towards Marie. That was ten years ago.

'I would have liked to go and sit on the bench with her and talk to her about all the things that had happened in the meantime,' he said. 'I didn't notice that that was the wish of a man in his fifties, who must have been strange to a young girl. It was only when I was sitting there on my own that it dawned on me. It still hurt, though; she would have had time. And the music in the church hurt as well, so that I fled and sat down in a bar in a part of town where we weren't staying. I was too drunk to go to the concert. I just felt like spending the evening on my own, I said over breakfast. Now she was the one who looked sad.'

26

AND THEN CAME the trip to Stockholm, a trip that would wipe out the whole of Scandinavia on Van Vliet's internal map.

It began with Lea's fear of flying, a fear she hadn't known before. She was pale, she was shaking and she needed to go to the lavatory.

'Afterwards it struck me as a particularly intelligent fear,' Van Vliet said. 'Gravity was her ally in the battle against her inner centrifugal forces. If she were raised from the ground there was a danger that Lea would shatter into pieces, that she would lose her inner centre, the scraps of her soul would go whirling in all directions and she would experience it as annihilation.

'That was my thought when we were sitting on the deck of the ferry on the way back. When Helsingborg sank back into the gloom, I wished the sun would never rise there again.

'"And if I suddenly can't remember how to go on?" Lea asked on the plane. And then she did something she had never done before: she told me about a conversation she had had with David Lévy.' She must have talked to him about her anxiety that her memory might leave her in the lurch. Van Vliet flinched when he heard that. He thought back to that moment that he had never forgotten: in the school hall, at Lea's first performance, when Lea had put the bow to the string and he had, for no reason, found himself wondering whether her memory would stand the strain. Lévy had looked mutely at Lea, before getting up and pacing back and forth in the music room. And then he had told her about the feelings that had assailed him in the most terrible moment of his life, when he had forgotten how to go on playing in the middle of the Oistrakh cadenza of Beethoven's violin concerto. Panic had flowed through him like an ice-cold, paralysing poison, he must have said. And even hours afterwards that poison had destroyed all other sensations. He couldn't remember having fled from the stage or how he had done it; all those movements – if he had even been aware of them – had been immediately expunged from his memory. He had looked at the Amati in the cloakroom and known: *never again*.

Up there above the clouds, Van Vliet had suddenly understood that the fear had connected his daughter with Lévy in a way that had made his own jealousy look shabby and ridiculous. It had been the solidarity of those who know that the loss of memory and self-confidence can – suddenly and without warning – leap out at you under the harsh spotlights, out of the darkness within. Now, all of a sudden, the father also understood how significant the gift of the Amati had been: Lévy had given Lea the violin to seal that dangerous darkness up within her for ever; and also so that she could continue, from within that sealed certainty, in inviolable, indestructible certainty, go on spinning his – Lévy's – notes, which had been simply interrupted and swallowed up by the inner void, and thus contribute to the healing of his old wound. And then she had wanted to smash that instrument, which contained within it such pain and hope, right in front of his eyes.

For the first time in ages, Van Vliet took her cold, moist hands in his. As he did so he thought of the fearful days and nights that had followed the outbreak of eczema. It was all far too much for them, just too much. When they stepped out into the arrivals hall, he wanted to suggest that she call off the concert and go home by ship and rail. But the chauffeur was already standing there.

'Why didn't I just send him away?' said Van Vliet. 'Just send him away!'

Dusk was falling. 'Shall I turn the light on?' I asked. Van Vliet shook his head. He didn't want to have any light on his face if he was going to talk about the disaster which seemed to me, when I finally heard it, like the climax of a tragedy towards which everything that had gone before was running with stern and unbending inevitability.

'When I was sitting in the darkness of the auditorium, I wished Lea hadn't talked about the collapse of Lévy's memory on the aeroplane. Because now at every moment I was waiting for her own. My gaze was fixed on her features, her eyes, always ready to recognize the first signs. It was a Mozart violin concerto; she wanted to get away from the identification with Bach. By now she had developed such a feeling for the Guarneri that the notes sounded a whole category fuller and more compelling than they had in the stairway. The newspapers had written about the Del Gesù; one of them had published a whole essay about it, also mentioning Paganini and *Il Cannone*. I think the respectful silence of the audience was a little greater than usual, and the applause was endless.

'As always, I was unsettled by the predictable, by-numbers quality of the way Lea took her ovations. But there was something else as well, and I think it shocked me to the core even though I didn't fully realize it at the time: Lea's movements when coming on and going off stage lacked her usual fluidity, they didn't flow at all the way human movements normally flow. Neither were they merely sluggish and prolonged. Instead there was something jerky about them, something pushed; a staccato, interrupted by tiny motionless hiatuses. It reminded me of the problems of motion in robots, which I knew from research that some colleagues had done. But it was *my daughter*!'

It was as if the silent horror that he hadn't really noticed before were only unfolding now, at a delay of several years. Van Vliet's voice changed and revealed the lava of emotions seething beneath. And if I think about the narrative of the next few hours, then I hear that roughness which expressed the pain that had scorched his soul better than any tears could.

'As regards the party after the concert, I don't remember much. Lea's movements were normal again, so that I almost forgot my earlier shock. Until I saw the splayed little finger when she took the cup. I don't know how to explain it, but it wasn't the affected splayed pinkie that one sees in an elegant, middle-class drawing room over afternoon tea. It was more of a misguided, pointless movement, a misrouted message from the nerve endings. I went to the lavatory and splashed cold water in my face. But instead of washing away the observation, I found myself remembering a failed trill during the concert. Trills had always been Lea's weak spot, and in one of those there had been a moment when it was as if her finger were making weird and incomprehensible movements. I pressed my forehead to the wall until it hurt. I had to rid myself of that damned hysteria!'

Van Vliet sank in on himself, the roughness vanished from his voice. 'If only it had been hysteria! A senseless, unfounded agitation!' he said quietly.

Something else had occurred to him over dinner: Lea's irritability. Recently she had often been irritable, particularly in the time after the break with Lévy. 'But what I now saw and sensed was different, more all-encompassing and physically urgent: as if she were burning.' Even in the car that took her to the hotel he could feel that burning, that suppressed fury that exuded from her like sweat.

'She was against me and also not. Do you understand? *Do you?*' he said.

The two last words came like a rough cry. I felt as if he were trying, years late, to pass on a part of Lea's fury to me, so that it would stop choking him. At the same time, that *you* was like the last, hoarse cry of help from someone being driven irrevocably out to sea by the ruthless current.

Against me and also not – that was the formula for his deepest despair, for guilt and loneliness, which had entered into a deadly, terrible bond with each other. *And also not* – you could feel him fighting with logic and illogic; a big, heavy Buster Keaton who wasn't making anyone laugh any more. He came out with the formula only once, but I heard and still hear the echo, that thousand-fold echo, that the words had within him. They were the melody that had drowned out everything else, simply everything, since Stockholm. A thought that never fell silent, not by day and not by night, either. An emotion that held within it everything that would happen next.

'The clerk at the hotel reception asked if she would play for him, just a few bars; unfortunately, he couldn't be at the concert. The top of his skull was unnecessarily flat and he wore a pair of glasses with an ugly fame; an awkward young man who had probably been preparing all day for this request. Perhaps, if he hadn't . . . But no, I've got to stop pretending. Otherwise it would have happened later anyway. It was inside her – whatever it was, yes, whatever it was. If I think about how it might have happened during the concert . . . How often I have dreamed about it since then! The dream raged within me, it consumed and toppled everything, it's as if I've been hollowed out.

'What I always feel in that dream: the chill of the cast-iron tip of the post at the bottom end of the banisters. When we had arrived, I had touched the grainy metal and thought: Like the top of a flight of steps in the Paris Metro. Now my eye fell once more on the metal tip, which grew like a snake's head from a conical construction of bulging metal. And from now on, you understand, I can no longer distinguish between genuine memory and internal images, which are manipulated and distorted by who knows what forces. If I close my eyes that metal point comes towards me with the violence of a fast zoom. And at the same time I have the feeling that I saw the approaching doom when Lea, hesitantly and with a surly expression, opened the violin case to comply with the young man's request. He walked timidly over to her, to get a closer look at the famous violin. Lea didn't let go of it, but he was allowed to run his hands over the lacquer. By now other employees had turned up and a few guests were standing expectantly in the lobby. Lea did a bit of quick tuning, but her movements were negligent, a careless routine. I thought she would start playing there, in the middle of the lobby. But that wasn't what happened, and the minutes that followed have stayed within me like a stretched film, stretched to tearing point. Once I dreamed I was cutting that film out of my head. If I lost my head in the process – it would still be better than having to watch that film over and over again.

'Lea walked to the stairs, lifted her long dress so as not to stumble, and stopped on the third step – yes, it was the third, exactly the third. She turned around and turned to her audience, so to speak. But she didn't look at us, her eyes were lowered, dark and distracted, it seemed to me. There was no reason for her not to start playing straight away. No discernible reason. A lighter clicked beside me. I turned violently around and peremptorily gestured to the man not to light his cigarette. Lea was looking straight ahead, like a soulless statue. It must have been prepared during those few seconds.

'At last she took the violin and began to play. It was the first few bars of the evening's Mozart Concerto. Suddenly she stopped, apparently mid-note. The interruption was so abrupt that the silence that followed was almost painful. For one brief moment I thought that was it, she'd had enough and wanted to go to bed. Or did I really think that? Even for a brief taster of her playing the interruption was too bizarre and abrupt, without any feeling for musical form. And the alienation in it was matched by the expression on Lea's face. Even on the way to the concert I had thought she had put on very pale make-up. She sometimes did that; we could never agree on that. And now, when she began to play again, that pale powder became the white mask of Loyola de Colón.

'Because Lea was playing, as she had done some time ago at home in the stairway, the music we had heard back then in Bern railway station. She played it as I had never heard her play before: furiously, with strokes of the bow that were so violent they scratched, one bow-hair after another tore, the white horsehairs whipped her face, it was a vision of defiance, despair and neglect, trickles of mascara ran down from behind her closed eyelids; now we could see the tears as well. Lea fought against them, one last fight. She was still a violinist who defended herself against the inner onslaught, with her fingers firmly on the strings, she pressed her lids against her eyeballs, pressed and pressed, the bow started sliding, the notes slid about, a woman beside me gasped, and then Lea, with her eyes full of tears, lowered the violin.

'It had hurt, and even now it hurts to see her standing there on the stairs, exhausted, defeated, destroyed. But it wasn't yet a disaster. A very few people had seen it and would put it down to exhaustion. *¡Pobrecita!* Someone behind me whispered.

'It was only when Lea lowered her bow and gripped the violin by the neck with both hands that I knew: It's over.'

Van Vliet stood up and walked to the window. He raised his arms, leaned forward and pressed his open palms against the glass. In that strange posture, supporting himself and yet looking as if he was trying to plunge through the glass into the depths below, in a rough and halting voice he described the event that he had wanted with all his strength to remove from his head.

'She pulled the violin high over her head, swung it backwards slightly to get a better run-up, and then she brought the back of it down on the metal point of the newel post. I wished she had at least closed her eyes as a sign that it hurt her somewhere deep within. But her gaze accompanied it all, the swing and the splintering, a gaze from eyes wide open and disturbed. And that was only the beginning. The back of the violin had burst open, the metal point had caught on the splintered edge of the opening, Lea tugged and levered; there were sounds of crunching and splintering; helpless rage transformed her features into a grimace. Now the violin was free again, then she pulled it up once more, and now she brought the bridge down on the metal point, the strings whirred and hummed, the bridge was shattered, the metal had drilled through one of the *f*-holes and torn it open.

'A man in a waiter's jacket stepped towards her and tried to stop her. He was the first one to overcome the general paralysis. I can't forgive myself for not getting to her first. She had managed to free the violin and swung it at the man like a weapon. He recoiled and let his arms dangle. Then Lea continued with her work of destruction: again and again she brought the smashed violin down on the metal, from in front and from behind, her hair stood up in a tangle from her head – no, she no longer looked like a Fury, that had only been for a moment; more and more she was a desperate little girl, breaking her toy out of rage and grief, shaken by sobs that were impossible to listen to, so that the people eventually walked away.

'The violin was stuck on the metal when Lea collapsed at last, slipped down a step and reached weakly for the newel post. It was only now that I managed to get to her, embraced her and ran my hand over her hair. The sobbing stopped. I hoped she might have at least a few moments of relaxed exhaustion. But her body had already stiffened again. I felt her already beginning to suffocate on what had happened, a suffocation that ate its way further and further inside her. When I saw her behind the woodpile in Saint-Rémy – and also when she appeared in the binoculars – I felt that stiffening, suffocating body in my arms.'

Meant for me and not for me. He didn't say it, but the silence in the room was full of it. Only now did I really understand how it must have felt for him when the doctor said: *C'est de votre fille qu'il s'agit*, and: *You're not moving to Saint-Rémy.*

During the night I tried to recreate part of the drama in my head. Leslie had painted for a while, quite well, and I had brought her painting materials at boarding school, and an easel too. When she grew slack I urged her to keep going and asked her on the telephone. I imagined what it would have been like if she had picked up the kitchen knife one day and shredded her paintings, above all the ones that I liked and had hung up in the office at the clinic. It was only fantasy, only a shadow, a breath compared to the paintings that Van Vliet had taken with him from the hotel in Stockholm. And yet it gave me gooseflesh.

'No more alcohol,' I said to him, and later gave him a sleeping pill. Like the Swedish doctor who gave Lea a tranquillizing injection. Van Vliet had sat by her bed all night. *This is the end.* Again and again that one thought, that internal rhythm, that sound of finality. The end of Lea's life with music. The end of his professional life, because now he had no way of paying back the embezzled money. The end of freedom, because eventually it would come to light. Was it also the end of her affection for him?

They were sitting at Marie's flat on the sofa with the chintz cushion. He was sitting with her at the kitchen table and heard her asking if she could go to Genoa and look at Paganini's violin. He held her in his arms before she went to her school leaving exam. He also thought about how they hadn't been able to draw up a list of guests when they wanted to celebrate her first full-size violin with a party. *I'd rather practise.* He also produced that sentence, which he later wanted to thrust into the dark gaze of the Maghrebi, along with Lea's tears of joy at the fair when she drew the gold ring. What had he done wrong? What did he have to reproach himself with? The wrong actions? The wrong feelings? Did such a thing even exist: right and wrong feeling? Feelings – weren't they just the way they were, full stop?

He had hired a car in Stockholm and driven home with Lea. She took some pills and slept a lot. When she was awake and their eyes met, that smile appeared on her face.

'The way you smile at someone towards whom you feel guilty, a guilt that can never be eradicated, a guilt that buries everything beneath it, and in that smile you reveal that you know as much. A smile that starts where all pleading for forgiveness stops. A smile as the only solution for not turning to stone.'

Sometimes he thought they were travelling in the wrong direction; a better choice would have been the north, Lapland, darkness, flight. Then again he wanted to forget that Scandinavia even existed. Putting the ruined fragments of the violin back together, splinter by splinter, and when the last one was reinserted into the old, immaculate form and covered with the magical lacquer whose composition must surely be well known: forget everything to do with that newel post and its snaky tip. Forget, just forget. They had come back to the hotel and calmly climbed the stairs. *Bonne nuit*, Lea had said. She always said that when they were travelling.

The boy with the ridiculous head and the ugly glasses had, they told him, spent hours creeping around on the floor searching for every splinter, even the smallest ones that had disappeared among the threads of the carpet. He hadn't been able to bear the thought that a violin by Guarneri del Gesù had been irrevocably destroyed.

Every now and again Van Vliet glanced at the back seat: the fragments hadn't fit properly into the violin case, and lay in a big plastic bag beside it. At rest stops his eye fell regularly on the dustbins. The bag bore the name of a Stockholm supermarket. That clue had to disappear. But it was impossible. Signor Buio had run his bony, liver-spotted hand over the violin before closing the lid and handing Van Vliet the shabby case.

'*Le violon*,' Lea sometimes murmured, half in her sleep. Then he ran his hand mutely over her shoulder and her arm. Since the disaster he hadn't managed to embrace her; he hadn't even stroked her hair. But at the same time he yearned to do so and was in despair about the paralysis forbidding it. When he had wiped the sweat from her forehead during the night, it had been the gesture of a nurse. Sometimes he had bent down to her to kiss her on the forehead. He hadn't managed to do it.

When he dozed off towards morning he was haunted by an image from a dream that he hadn't shaken off even now: the boy from hotel reception was trying in vain to free the skewered violin from the newel post. He pulled and tugged and twisted, it crunched and groaned and splintered. He couldn't do it. He simply couldn't do it.

He had stood for a long time by the railing on the ferry, looking into the night, before reaching for the phone and calling his sister Agnetha. We had been together for three days now, three long days of storytelling, during which we had slipped through thirteen years and he had never once mentioned his sister. It had always sounded as if he were an only child.

'Why, damn it all, must she have that Swedish name of all names? People always said: ABBA! And ABBA didn't even exist in 1955. It was some fashion model in a magazine that made my mother think of it. She was addicted to the gossip in the glossy magazines. "Imagine: not Agnes and not Agatha, no: *Agnetha*!" she said.

'That was before their marriage broke down and love plunged from the stars into the dust. When my father later related the episode, he took my mother's hand, deformed by gout, and then you could sense that the stars had once existed. And that was why there was always a shimmer of starlight on Agnetha, a bit of gold dust, as if she had a fine, invisible strand of gold in her hair. But there's nothing radiant about her. She has always been a sound, unimaginative, hard-working girl who didn't like my anarchism and immoderation. "You're a steamroller," she would say. Of course, she thought I was an inadequate father, so that I wanted to prove the opposite to her.

'That was why it was hard to call her now. I didn't mention the violin. Breakdown – that was enough.

'"Dr Meridjen," she said immediately. "We need to get Lea out of the country, away from the press. He's good, very good, and the clinic has an excellent reputation, and she'll also be in the French language, Cécile's language, I think that's important."

'She's a clinical psychologist and has worked with the Maghrebi in Montpellier. She's always admired him, and maybe even more than that.

'She had herself well under control when she saw Lea, but she was shocked. She asked to see the pills that the Swedish doctor had given her, and shook her head irritably. I hadn't seen my sister for years and was amazed at the maturity and competence expressed by everything about her. She wanted to know everything. I just said it had been a valuable violin.

'Lea slept. We were sitting in the kitchen. Agnetha saw how exhausted I was after the long journey. A few hours in a motel was all I'd had.

'"What do we know about these things!" I said.

'"Yes," she said. Then she stepped behind me, her brother, who crushed everything in his path with his arrogance, and put her arms around my neck.

'"Martijn," she said. Afterwards she was the only one who stood by me.'

What do we know? Before, as part of the narrative, those words had been stressed with the controlled detachment of the storyteller. Now they exploded from him roughly and impetuously.

'What, damn it all, do we know? They all act as if they know what's happened. Agnetha, the Maghrebi. I've even heard this nonsense from my colleagues. We know nothing about these things! *Nothing!*'

He was sitting in an armchair. Now he leaned forwards, rested his elbows on his knees and let his head dangle as if into the void. He was shaken by a dry sob; sometimes it sounded like coughing. His despair discharged itself in an uncontrollable, animal quivering and twitching. I wanted to do what Agnetha had done, when she stepped behind him. But it was impossible not to do anything. In the end I knelt on the floor in front of him and drew his head into my arms. It took a few minutes for the shaking to calm down and finally ebb away. I pulled him up by the shoulders until he was sitting straight in his chair. I have seen a lot of sick and exhausted people. But this – this was something else. I wish I could erase the image of his head falling against the back of the armchair.

27

I LEFT THE CONNECTING DOOR ajar and the light on. Then I went down to the hotel library as I had done the previous night. *I have been one acquainted with the night. / . . . I have outwalked the furthest city light. / I have looked down the saddest city lane.* Apart from Whitman and Auden, Robert Frost was the third poet that Liliane had shown me. *And miles to go before I sleep.* She had been furious that all these lines, when spoken, sounded like hackneyed phrases from a pop song. '*Poetry*,' she had said, '*is a strictly solitary affair; solipsistic, even. I ought not to talk to you about it. But . . . well . . .* '

A nurse who knew the word *solipsistic*. Why, Liliane, did you have to die in that accident? You could have wiped the sweat from my brow even in India. I tried to walk with her through the winter dawn of Boston and hear her saying *grand*, her Irish accent. It didn't work. Everything was pallid, lifeless, far away. Instead I felt Martijn van Vliet's head in my arms and smelled the bitter odour of his ruffled hair.

I was afraid of what was to come. *Afterwards she was the only one who stood by me.* When they brought him up before the judge, it couldn't mean anything else.

And then Lea's death. Wasn't Stockholm already enough? More than anyone could bear? *That was my last trip to Saint-Rémy . . . Yes, I think it was the last trip.* Was the interpretation still open?

I had to prevent it. Did I *have to*? *Could* I, even? Where incurable illnesses were concerned – there I had a clear and unshakeable opinion. A matter of dignity. But how did that apply here?

It was nearly midnight. I still called Paul. 'If someone simply can't go on,' I said, 'simply can't go on . . . ' I was speaking in riddles, he thought. Was everything all right?

Why did I have no friends? People who could slip without guidance into the world of my thoughts and understood without explanation? What had Liliane said? *I hate patronizing.* But it wasn't about patronizing anyone. What *exactly* was it about?

I called Leslie. She had been sleeping and wanted to have a coffee first. She had sounded tense and I had thought it was annoyance. But when she called back she sounded composed and for a moment I thought she was happy that I had called.

If someone simply can't go on, she said, you have to let them do what they must, and even help them. She was talking about patients and I was glad that we had reached the same opinion independently. But this was about something else. Tragedy . . . Well, yes, she said, you could help someone to overcome it . . . but of course I knew that myself . . .

How could I have expected anyone to say anything beyond platitudes? Anyone who hadn't held Van Vliet's head in his hands?

Leslie was unhappy when she sensed my disappointment. 'The day before yesterday, questions about boarding schools and instruments, and now . . . '

I was glad we were talking to each other more often, I said.

28

WITHOUT LEA the flat was empty, and that emptiness sometimes came towards Van Vliet on the stairs. Then he turned around and went to eat. And drink.

He could barely endure the silence either. None the less he didn't hear a single note of music for a whole year. Films were also impossible, there was music in them. He usually watched television with the sound off. The emptiness and the silence – he sensed it, even though he couldn't have explained it – were related to the bleaching that had afflicted Lea on her last visit to Marie, and which he had seen before him once again when walking to Signor Buio's at night. Sometimes his office bleached out, too, usually at nightfall. The light meant that it was impossible, but it was still the case. If someone had come in at such moments, he might have shot them. That was only one of many things that estranged him from himself. Cross-country skiing in the Oberland did him good. But he went there only when he was sure: he wouldn't do it. There was no question of leaving Lea in the lurch. In spite of the Maghrebi. Partly because of him.

Over breakfast Van Vliet showed no sign of what had happened in the night. He was freshly shaven. He was wearing a dark blue fisherman's pullover and looked healthy and athletic, like a holidaymaker, slightly tanned. Not at all like someone who preferred to let someone else take the tiller. He had the relaxed face of someone who had been able to flee his worries in a deep sleep. I didn't know if the sleeping pill had washed away the memory of the collapse. Whether he remembered me holding him.

Afterwards we sat by the lake again. We would leave today, we both sensed that. But not until he had brought his story into the present. Above the lake there lay a winter light without the brilliance and promise of Provence. A light that contained grey slate, cold white and merciless sobriety. The fog began towards Martigny, light at first, compact and impenetrable further back. It took my breath away to imagine that I was to drive into it.

By now Van Vliet's sentences were curt and laconic. Sometimes he lapsed into an analytical, almost academic tone, as if he were talking about someone else. Perhaps, I thought, it was also to allow him to forget the nocturnal dissolution, the loss of all contours. I wasn't unhappy about it. But there was also something menacing about his self-control, something oppressive that matched the approaching fog.

Agnetha had driven Lea to Saint-Rémy. He was glad of that, but unhappy about the feeling. Her eyes had been dull and her lids heavy when he had stroked her hair as he said goodbye. When the car pulled up she sat in her seat like a plaster doll, her empty gaze staring straight ahead.

He collected Nikki from the kennel. The dog was delighted and jumped up at him. But he missed Lea and wouldn't eat properly. He slowly got used to the new rhythm of life. He was allowed to sleep beside Van Vliet's bed. Except he couldn't bear those long hours on his own, so Van Vliet took him into the Institute. Ruth Adamek hated dogs. When they had to discuss something, they spoke on the phone across the corridor. Another colleague, on the other hand, was wild about Nikki. When the dog licked her hand it gave Van Vliet a pang.

After six months he drove to see Lévy in Neuchâtel and discovered how Lea had tried to smash the Amati when he introduced her to his fiancée.

Van Vliet spoke curtly and soberly about what had happened in Stockholm.

'Back then it was aimed at me,' said Lévy, 'but now . . . '

The two very different men were feeling their way towards each other. Van Vliet was reminded of the Oistrakh cadenza.

'I have never had a pupil more gifted than Lea,' said Lévy. 'I couldn't resist the temptation to work with her. The danger – I refused to see it. Do you think . . . ?'

For days Van Vliet thought about what Lévy had wanted to ask. He still didn't like the man and felt clodhopping and clumsy when he was around him. But he was no longer the adversary he had once been. '*Je suis désolé, vraiment désolé,*' he had said in the doorway. Van Vliet had believed him. They had waved to one another, only briefly, almost shamefacedly. On the station platform Van Vliet had had the peculiar feeling: now Neuchâtel is empty too.

He avoided Krompholz. But then he met Katharina Walther in the street by chance. 'My God,' she said again and again. 'My God.' He didn't look at her, instead speaking down at her shoes.

'They had . . . ' he said at last.

'But no one could have guessed that!' she interrupted.

As they hugged goodbye her chignon brushed his nose.

Much later, when they had learned of the embezzlement, he met her again. She didn't let him slip by. It was a strange look that she gave him, he would cling to it for a long time.

'When I read about it: My God, I thought, he did everything for her, really *everything*. I . . . I too would have liked to have someone who . . . I can still feel it in my hand, even today, the del Gesú.'

'Me too,' he had said.

After that they didn't meet up again before the cemetery.

29

IT STAYED A SECRET for just over a year. Van Vliet postponed projects, sabotaged experiments, dragged out purchases and left bills unpaid. When the sponsors got in touch he lied without restraint. When he talked about it, his face adopted the expression that I knew by now: the gambler, the boy who wanted to be a forger. Deliberate obstruction, planned incompetence – he was dancing over the abyss. The abyss made its appearance at night. He'd liked it, in a way. There was a hint of that pleasure in his voice. When I became aware of it, I thought of the inner layers and plateaux he had spoken of in Lea.

I wished, Martijn, that the gambler within you could have saved you. Could have built a platform inside you, on which you could have gone on living.

There was more fear than pleasure involved when Van Vliet noticed that Ruth Adamek was on his heels. Once when he surprised her by stepping into her room, he saw that she was trying out passwords on his research account. IRENRAUG it said on the screen. As a schoolboy he had broken all records when it came to reading words backwards. Sooner or later she would plainly be trying DELGESÚ. That wouldn't be enough. But once she had started, she would go on switching the letters round and round. That was what they had done in the first year of their collaboration, when they needed to reconstruct a forgotten password for which they knew only the starting point. It had been summer and she had sat in her short skirt on the edge of his desk. The letters game had become a competition which she had won. From the corner of his eye he had seen her slowly running her tongue along her lips. Now or never. He had stared fixedly at the screen until the moment had passed. 'By the way,' she had said to him the next day, 'you're a lousy loser.'

He changed the password to ANOMERC, later that turned into CRANEMO, but that sounded too much like CREMONA, so it turned into OANMERC.

'Why did I stick to that subject? Why didn't I choose something less obvious? Or at least BUIO or OIUB or something that she would never have been able to guess.'

'What we know about compulsive actions,' Agnetha said, 'is that they are based on a hidden desire that the very thing that is feared might happen.'

He thought that was incredibly clever. But what surprised him was that he had remained with the topic of betrayal, as if he stuck to it.

Then, three years ago, the letter arrived in which the sponsors demanded detailed accounts or else they would not be in a position to allow the promised money to go on flowing. 'I opened it by accident,' said Ruth Adamek, when she handed him the letter. He looked at the sender's name. Time for the showdown. 'Put it somewhere, anywhere,' he said nonchalantly and left.

In the station he stood for a while on the spot from which they had listened to Loyola de Colón. Fifteen years had passed since then. He took the train to the Oberland. It looked like snow, but none was falling. On the way back he wondered what he would have done. She was with the Maghrebi, behind the woodpile, what difference did it make? The doctor had looked at him in silence when he asked if Lea had asked after him. That black, sealed gaze, that medical complacency. He wanted to thump him.

He took sick leave and didn't go to the institute for a week. Let them all read the letter. It didn't matter any more.

During those days he cleared the flat, picked up every object. He took out the photograph that showed Cécile's room before they had turned it into *la chambre de musique*. The past that came towards him then caught him with unexpected force. For the first time he wondered what Cécile would have thought about his fraud. *Martijn, the romantic cynic! I didn't think there really was such a thing!* And now he had driven across half of

Europe, not to his beloved wife, but with his sick daughter beside him. In the motel they had acted as if he were her lover. When he woke up next to her, even more dejected than before, she had been breathing calmly, but her eyelids were twitching uneasily. 'Where are we?' she had said. 'Why didn't the agency book me a better room? Normally I have a suite.'

Lea's room was the last one he cleared. He had avoided doing it. Now here, too, he took everything in hand, as he had done last time. Layers of a life story. Cuddly toys, the first drawings, school reports. A diary with a lock. He found the key. He decided against it and pushed the book right to the back of the drawer. The Maghrebi had asked about such things. '*Absolument pas*,' he had said.

LEA LÉVY. He threw the notebook away. Mountains of portraits. She had had her photograph taken many times recently. He sat down with the pictures at the kitchen table. LEA VAN VLIET. Something behind the façade had started to crumble, silently and inexorably. He fetched pictures from former times and gauged the distance. One he had taken shortly after Loyola's performance at the railway station. In it Lea looked as she had done when she dragged him through the city, impelled by that new will that later led to the question: *Is a violin expensive*? Most of the pictures of Lea, the glamorous violinist, he threw away. He didn't know why, but he locked Lea's room and put the key in the kitchen cupboard, behind the crockery that he seldom used.

When he had made up his mind what he was going to do, he invited Caroline along. Her breathing was heavy and she sometimes closed her eyes as he told his story. Someone would have to look after the flat, he said. She nodded and stroked Nikki. 'You're coming with me,' she said. There were tears in her eyes. 'She must never find out,' she said. He nodded.

He guessed that she had something else that she wanted to say to him. Something that only friends say to each other. He was afraid of it.

There had been that boy, two classes above her, in spite of his smoking the best athlete of his year, a poser, a pocket James Dean but a heart-throb to many of the girls.

Van Vliet felt panic rising up in him. Might he, her father, have stood in her way? He hung on Caroline's lips.

Then she, more than thirty years his junior, took his hand.

'No,' she said, 'no, not at all. Not you. It was her unapproachability, if you like. The aura of her talent and her success. Whether in the classroom or the playground. There was always that cool halo around her. A bit of envy, a bit of fear, a bit of incomprehension, everything all together. She didn't know how to step out of that halo, out to Simon, for example. Her halo followed her like a shadow. And Simon – he never looked at her, but he gazed after her, there was giggling. But even for him, the cock of the walk, she was out of range, simply too far away. "You know," she said, "sometimes I wish all the glitter and glamour would vanish overnight, so that the others would be normal towards me, quite normal."'

Van Vliet hesitated. And Lévy? he asked at last.

'David – he was something different, something *completely* different. I don't know. He was reaching for the stars.'

Simon and Lévy?

'As far as she was concerned they had nothing to do with each other. They were two different worlds, I would say.'

There was something else that Van Vliet wanted to know, something he had been wondering for a long time.

'First music was connected with Marie, then with Lévy. It always had to do . . . with love.' Did Lea simply love music – I mean, for its own sake?

Caroline had never asked herself that question. 'I don't know,' she said. 'No, I really don't know. Sometimes . . . No, no idea.'

Once again she gazed into the distance as if she wanted to tell him something about Lea that he couldn't know. But then she looked at him and said something which I think spared Van Vliet a great deal: 'I'll ask Dad to take on your defence. He's good on cases like yours, very good.'

He hugged her as they said goodbye and held her for a moment too long, as if she were Lea. Caroline wiped the tears from her eyes as she left.

The next morning he went to the Prosecutors' Office.

30

HE DIDN'T TELL ME much about the investigation and the trial. Between his sparse sentences he threw bits of bread to the swans. A man like him in the dock: there wasn't much to explain. As he threw the bread, I had the feeling he was taking care not to be sucked into the maelstrom of memory; to glide away over it unharmed.

The investigating magistrate, whose job it was to test the credibility of his statement, focused on two things: the motive and the circumstance that neither the violin nor a receipt for its purchase could be presented. 'There were moments when he looked at me with an expression that suggested I was a lunatic or a hardened liar.' For a long time Van Vliet refused to dig out the remains of the violin. What he didn't reveal – not even to the court – was the true story of its destruction. He himself had trodden on it in the dark – nothing more could be enticed from him.

I see you sitting in the courtroom, Martijn – a man who could stay silent like a great stone wall.

The investigating magistrate wanted to question Lea. Van Vliet must have lost his composure at that point. Dr Meridjen wrote an assessment. Van Vliet dreamed that the doctor told her about it. After that he sat on the edge of his bed and hammered his head with his fists, dinning into himself the insight that no doctor would do such a thing, ever.

Caroline's father managed to get him a lenient sentence, not least because Van Vliet had confessed. Eighteen months on probation. The judge must have found it easier to understand the motive. Part of her task – she must have said – was judging how difficult it would have been for him not to do what he had done. Van Vliet said only one word: *Impossible.*

Eventually someone must have dropped the phrase 'psychiatric assessment'. The two words sounded hoarse when Van Vliet spoke about it. A dangerous hoarseness. Then he mutely pursed and unpursed his lips, pursed and unpursed. For a while he forgot to throw the bits of bread to the swans and crumbled them between his fingers.

Of course he lost his professorship. The sponsors saw to it that his remaining funds were impounded. What he was left with was enough for the two-room flat in which he now lived, and he was also able to keep his car. Caroline's father helped him in his battle with medical insurance. At the end he persuaded them to shoulder the cost of Lea's stay in Saint-Rémy.

The newspapers wrote in big letters, they came at him from every corner, bold and brutal. He walked absently through the city and bought up all the copies so that Lea wouldn't get to see them.

'During that time I played against the old man in Cremona, again and again. At last I found a solution. The problem was: I don't accept sacrifices. I assume from the outset that every gambit is a trap that you mustn't think about any further. That was how it was back then. I should have taken the damned bishop. The old man had miscalculated and I also discovered why. I should have taken him with my pawn. Now I moved my pawn over and thought: That one movement, an inch, an inch and a half – and I wouldn't be here in court.

'Mother used to laugh when Father, violently reproaching himself, said that he could *disencrypt* himself; she found the expression hysterical. Now it occurred to me too: sometimes I was so furious with myself that I felt as if I were almost losing my mind. The worst thing was when I said to myself: You basically didn't do it for Lea, you did it for yourself. You travelled to see the old man because you fell into the trap of the gambler, out of self-infatuation.'

He said he wanted to go for a short walk on his own and looked at me apologetically. I knew: the worst was yet to come.

31

'As a little child Lea was impressed by the brown glass containers with the handwritten labels that stood on the shelves in the chemist's shop. She even drew the jars. They must have had a mysterious power of attraction for her; perhaps because behind the dark glass you could see the bright powder that looked as if it was hidden, promising or even dangerous. Later she once saw Cécile locking the special medicine cabinet in the hospital. "That's the poison cupboard," Cécile explained. Lea must have been very impressed with the phrase, because over dinner she asked: "Why would they need poison in hospital?"

'I thought about that when I learned of her death. She did it during the night shift.'

A year ago she had come back from Saint-Rémy. She had called not him, but Agnetha. It had hurt; on the other hand, he was glad that she didn't see his shabby flat. He had come up with various explanations as he lay awake in bed. None of them sounded believable. But he would never reach the truth all by himself. He realized to his horror that he was afraid of bumping into his daughter.

She started training as a nurse and lived in the nurses' home. It was at the other end of the city. He lived in the same city as his daughter and he still hadn't seen her. Agnetha gave him the number. 'I'd wait until she calls,' she said.

For fear of meeting her he didn't dare go into the centre for the first few weeks. 'I lived as if something inside me were pressing hard on me. I think my breathing was very shallow. Like someone ashamed of his very existence. It only dawned on me very slowly: behind my back the shame of fraud and condemnation had turned into a feeling of guilt towards Lea. But there *was* no such guilt!

'I became furious: with the Maghrebi, who had persuaded her of God alone knows what; with Agnetha, because of her remark; even with Caroline, who thought it was better not to give back the dog. And I became furious with Lea, more and more each day. Why – damn it all to hell – didn't she call? Why was she behaving as if I had done something to her?'

It was last autumn when they finally met. A warm day, people were lightly clad. That was why the first thing he noticed was her stiff, modest suit and her severe hairdo. He didn't recognize her immediately. He caught his breath: less than two years had passed since he last saw her through his binoculars in Saint-Rémy, and she looked as if at least twice as much time had gone by. Clear eyes behind rimless glasses, the whole appearance not without elegance, but unapproachable, terribly unapproachable.

Slowly they took the last steps towards one another. They shook hands. 'Dad,' she said. 'Lea,' he said.

Van Vliet stepped to the shore, scooped a handful of water and let it run down his face.

I felt myself slumping. I didn't want to hear anything more of this sorry tale. I didn't have the strength.

They had stepped out together on to the Minster Terrace and stood side by side in silence for a while.

'I can never make up for it,' she said suddenly.

A great weight fell from him. For the first time in months he was able to take a deep breath. *That* was why, only that was why she had been avoiding him. And she didn't know anything about fraud and the guilty verdict, she talked only about the violin. He wanted to hug her, but paused before he could. Her voice had sounded as it always did. But otherwise she felt strange to him; not forbidding and not cold, but rather limp; like someone just ticking over.

'It's fine,' he said. 'Everything's fine.'

She looked at him like someone who has said something forced or unbelievable to provide reassurance.

Sitting on a bench they had a brief conversation about where and how they were living now. He must have lied.

She asked if there had been anything about it in the papers. He was glad, because it showed that she was back in the real world and in real time. He shook his head.

'Stockholm,' she said, and after a while. 'After that, darkness, complete darkness.'

He took her hand. She put up no resistance. Later he felt her head on his shoulder. That opened the floodgates. Wrapped in a clumsy embrace, they both gave their tears free rein.

After that he waited for her call. It didn't come. He tried to call her, again and again. He would have loved to know what Saint-Rémy had been like for her. And also so that the images of her behind the woodpile and on the wall, her arms wrapped around her knees, which had flowed together in his mind into icons of loneliness and despair, could liquefy and turn into episodes that blurred into the past and lost their horrors.

The call from the hospital came in the small hours of the morning. Three days before, a trainee from the nurses' home had shown Lea old newspaper reports about the trial. After that she had appeared for work as usual, laconic, but then she always was. Now she lay there, her white face as irrevocably still as Cécile's had been.

'Since then,' Van Vliet said, 'everything has been empty. Empty and bleached.'

He waited, without knowing what for. At last he borrowed money from Agnetha to take this trip.

32

ON THE WAY TO BERN I kept thinking of the words he had added: 'And now I've met you.'

It might have been a grateful observation, nothing more than that. And it might have been more: an announcement that he wanted to cling to this anchor and go on living.

As I had done throughout all those days, I was worried about our arrival. Would it resolve the contradiction between the two interpretations? Would I be strong and firm enough to be his anchor? I felt myself giving Paul the scalpel. Could one be an anchor for someone else – for someone who had ceased to trust his own hands?

We stopped outside my flat. Van Vliet studied the elegant façade in silence. We shook hands. 'Let's be in touch,' I said.

Dry words after all that had happened. But on the steps nothing better occurred to me.

I lifted the shutters and opened the windows. And I saw him. He had driven a few houses further on and parked. Now he was sitting in the gloom with the lights off. *La nuit tombe.* He liked those words. They still connected him with Cécile. There were no lorries for him to fear. He didn't want to go home. I thought about how the void had come towards him when he climbed the stairs after Lea left.

I'd actually like to see where you live, I said when he wound down the window. 'It isn't a flat like yours,' he said, 'but then you know that.'

I was, in fact, startled by the shabbiness of his rooms. He hadn't had the money to have it repainted. There were shadows on the walls where paintings had once been. In the kitchen there were pipes that protruded from the wall and then entered it again somewhere else, flaking paint, an antediluvian oven. Only the chairs and carpets recalled the flat of a scientist on a decent salary. And the bookshelves. I looked for them and found them, the books about Louis Pasteur and Marie Curie. He saw my face and smiled wanly. Technical literature all the way up to the ceiling. A rack of records. A lot of Bach with Itzhak Perlman. 'He set the standard for Lea,' he said. 'The record from Cremona with the different violin tones.' Miles Davis. In one corner a violin case. 'They didn't think about that one. I could sell it to the violin-maker in St Gallen. But then I would be left with nothing of her.'

He stood as if paralysed in his own flat, unable even to sit down. When he had seen Lea standing motionless at the window of her room in Saint-Rémy and looking out across the landscape, he had thought that she felt completely alien on this planet. That occurred to me now that I saw him standing there.

I put on Miles Davis. He turned out the light. When the last note had faded away I stood up in the darkness, touched his shoulder and left the room without a word. I have never felt closer to anyone.

33

TWO DAYS LATER he called. We walked along the Aare, a silent memory of the beach at Saintes Maries de la Mer and the shore of Lake Geneva. He asked questions about my job, about Leslie's work in Avignon, and finally, hesitantly, he asked what my life would be like now.

I would have been glad of his questions had they not been so distanced. *Detached*, as Liliane said. Likewise his handshake when he said goodbye, and his absent nod when I suggested taking another walk. Had he already finished? Or is that only the shadow that later knowledge casts on former events?

On the bus home I imagined the rice fields of the Camargue and the drifting clouds. If only we'd stayed down there, I thought, and allowed ourselves to drift, two shadows against the light. I printed the photographs and leaned the picture of Martijn, the one in which he is drinking, against the lamp.

The next day it snowed. I thought of his trips to the Oberland. I was worried and called again and again, in vain. The next morning I was flicking through a newspaper. A red Peugeot with Bern number plates had crossed into the opposite lane on a road in the Bernese Seeland and crashed head-on into a lorry. The driver had been killed instantly. 'It was very tight, he must have braked to let me past, and he went into a skid,' the driver had said. 'He looked curiously calm behind the wheel, he must have been paralysed with horror.'

All day I saw his hands in front of me: quivering on the horse's head, floating about the wheel, on the bedcovers.

By the grave I was alone with Agnetha. 'Martijn doesn't make mistakes when he's driving,' she said.

There was defiant pride in her voice, and it went far beyond driving. He loved snow, she said. Snow and the sea, ideally both at once.

34

FROM THE CEMETERY I went to the house where Marie Pasteur had lived. The brass plaque was no longer there, just the traces on the cast-iron door. I looked along the street that Lea had taken by mistake after her last visit, and which had, in her father's mind, become an endless, fading straight line.

The metal point on the newel post in Stockholm had flown at Van Vliet with the violence of a fast zoom. The image began to pursue me. I went to the cinema to get over it. The film images helped, but I didn't want to see those film images, and left again shortly afterwards.

After that I had to drive, feel the motion of the car, it made it easier. I took the bus back and forth through the city, from one end to the other and back, and then the same on the next stretch. I thought of *Thelma and Louise* and the two pairs of women's hands, and how Van Vliet had loved their foolhardy grace. When the bus emptied I closed my eyes and imagined I was sitting at the wheel and driving to Hammerfest and Palermo in search of those images of one final freedom. With each bus I was less sure that I was only driving towards the images. I felt more and more as if I were driving the bus towards the edge of the canyon.

As I waited in vain for sleep at home, I felt that I couldn't simply go on with my life. There is unhappiness of a dimension so great that it is unbearable. And so, at dawn, I began to write what I had experienced since that bright, windy morning in Provence.